Love's Harvest

By

Linda Shenton Matchett

To Susan Shenton Greger,

whose gentle spirit and deep faith

are so like Ruth's.

I love you, Sis.

"Later, Naomi's sons married Moabite women.

One was named Orpah and the other Ruth." (Ruth 1:4)

Volga Region, Russia, 1923

Chapter One

"We'll die if we don't leave this place. Pack only what you can carry." Edmund Hirsch poked his bony arms into the sleeves of his wool coat that sported more holes than Swiss cheese. A paroxysm of coughing gripped his body, the result of a mustard gas attack on his German platoon nine years ago during The Great War.

After several minutes the coughing ceased, and he mopped the sweat from his forehead with a dingy, gray handkerchief. "Be ready. We set out tomorrow at first light."

"Where will we go, *Vati*?" Five-year-old Conrad's voice trembled.

"Don't be a baby, Conrad." Older by two minutes, Conrad's twin brother, Manfred, finished tying his boot laces and jumped off the chair, his shoes clomping against the bare wood floor. His bright blue eyes blazed above his hollow cheeks.

"Hush, children." Noreen stroked Conrad's white-blond hair and met her husband's terse look with one of her own. "You heard your father. There's no time to waste."

***

Noreen yanked the zipper closed on her over-stuffed canvas satchel. Always resourceful, Edmund had attached straps to the moss-green bag so she could wear it on her back. She would also carry a suitcase in each hand. The journey promised to be arduous.

Sighing, she wiped a weary hand across her dry eyes. Even if she had any tears remaining, crying was useless. It would not make their situation less dire.

Muted voices and the occasional bump filtered through the ceiling from the boys' bedroom above. Noreen shivered and hunched into her threadbare, ruby-red sweater. An impulse purchase made during her honeymoon, the garment held more memories than warmth. Edmund insisted it brought out the roses in her cheeks.

She tossed the bulging satchel to the floor and turned her attention to the yawning luggage on the bed. Two steel pots and a fry pan nestled in the bottom of one boxy, brown suitcase between faded blue towels that had been a belated wedding present from her mother and father.

Hopefully, Edmund would find somewhere they could live in his home country with enough food to actually cook. Here, along the

Volga River in Russia, the crops had failed again, and the famine was entering its second year. The decision whether to eat or plant their seed wheat had caused many families to die of starvation.

Shuffling footsteps sounded behind her. She turned as Edmund enveloped her in his arms. Nestling against his too-thin chest, she breathed in his musky scent. He bent and kissed her forehead, his black beard scraping her skin.

"You work too hard." He tucked a stray strand of her nutmeg-colored hair behind her ear.

She leaned into his touch. "Isn't that why you married me?"

"No, *Schatzi,* it is most certainly not." He grinned. "You stole my heart. I had to marry you, or I would die a broken man."

"Don't joke about that. Our friends are dying every day." She frowned. "Who knew this famine would last so long? If it weren't for the bit of help arriving from America's Volga Relief Society, matters would be much worse."

"They are sending more assistance than we are receiving. Jakob told me there is proof the government is confiscating some of the packages and keeping the money to construct new buildings and conduct repairs. As always, development of the country is valued above the lives of the people."

"Shhh!" She pressed the work-worn fingers of her right hand against his lips. "You could get in trouble for saying that. Then where would we be?"

Edmund hugged her. "There is no one to hear us, but I understand your fear. Many unexplained disappearances make for extreme caution." He released her and gestured toward the pile of clothes on their bed. "Enough depressing talk. What can I do to help?"

"Do you have our passports? With the government ratcheting up the price, we have no more savings to purchase new ones."

"Now who's speaking out against the authorities?" He patted the breast pocket of his coat. "I have the passports and our traveling papers safe and sound."

"Good." Noreen waved him away. "Then go see what the boys are about. I gave explicit instructions about what to pack, but they have a mind of their own." She shook her head. "Well, Manfred does. Conrad simply tags along."

He kissed the tip of her nose and raised his hand in mock salute. "*Jawohl!*"

She giggled and pushed him out of the room. Closing the door behind him, she sobered and dropped to her knees next to the bed. "Dear Heavenly Father, thank You for Edmund. He is a good man.

Give him strength for the journey and keep us safe as we travel. Soften the hearts of his family so they will welcome us home."

Home.

Berlin was Edmund's home. Not hers.

English born and bred, Noreen stroked the floral bedspread as visions of daffodils in Regents Park flitted through her head, their golden yellow blooms swaying in the breeze. Big Ben soaring into the sky. Tower Bridge spanning the River Thames. Pristine white swans fishing the waters of Serpentine Lake in Hyde Park where a chance meeting changed the trajectory of her life.

In an effort to heal his damaged lungs, Edmund moved to London after the war. Someone told him the damp English air would act as a balm. A lover of art, he had attended the Spring Festival where she sat under a tent selling her baskets.

She climbed to her feet, and her gaze sought out the willow basket on their dresser. The basket Edmund purchased when he returned to her booth after taking his girlfriend home. His last date with the woman.

Noreen's smile broadened. Who knew basket weaving would catch her a husband? She flushed as she remembered the conversation.

"If I purchase this basket, will you go out with me?"

"What about your girlfriend?"

"I told her we were finished, that I was going to marry you."

"Isn't that a bit rash? You don't even know me."

"I know enough."

After a whirlwind courtship, Edmund asked for her hand in marriage. Her parents objected, so Edmund took her to the register office where he wed her in front of two gray-haired, bored-looking clerks. A year later the twins were born, and her parents decided being grandparents was more important than holding a grudge. They eventually grew to love their German son-in-law as much as their daughter did. Enough to support the family's move to Russia in another effort to heal Edmund's lungs. She swallowed against the lump in her throat. Her parents' death last year in a train accident still stung.

Overheard, a thump followed by laughter broke her reverie. Warmth filled her. She loved her country, but she loved Edmund more. That is why she would leave all but her most necessary possessions and travel to yet another foreign country to live with her in-laws. People she had never met who spoke a language she didn't know.

Berlin, Germany, 1931

Chapter Two

Noreen stood and stared out the window. The April rains thrummed against the windowpanes blurring the view to a kaleidoscope of colors. Behind her, Edmund coughed in his fevered sleep. His condition had worsened since arriving at his parent's home.

She turned toward him and dropped into the chair next to the bed. Pressing her hand to his forehead, she held her breath. His skin was clammy and hot. She stroked his cheek, and he moaned. His hands gripped the covers, and his head jerked away from her touch.

"It's okay, Edmund. I'm here." Reaching into the bucket on the floor, she wrung out the small towel soaking in the water. She laid the cool cloth on his brow, and he sighed. His breath rattled in his chest.

Won't you heal him, Heavenly Father? He served his country, and he served you. Our boys need their father. Are those reasons enough to warrant Your mercy, or is there some promise You are trying to extract from me? I will do anything for You, if You'll save my husband.

Thunder rumbled. Lightning flashed.

Noreen jumped to her feet and peered outside at the sky. *Is that You, Lord? Are You trying to tell me something?*

Footsteps pounded on the stairs. The door flew open, and Conrad stood in the entryway. His blond hair spiked around his face. His wide-eyed gaze flew to the motionless form of his father.

"*Mutti? Großmutter* says Thor is coming for *Vati*. She says the storm is his way of covering his tracks."

"That's nonsense." Noreen clamped her lips shut and held out her arms. Conrad crossed the room in a flash and grasped her in a stifling hug. Her mother-in-law's superstitions had given her son many a nightmare over the years, but she shouldn't denigrate Edmund's mother.

Noreen stroked Conrad's back and listened to her son's broken words. "But *Vati* is going to die, isn't he? Maybe not tonight, but soon. He's not getting any better, and the doctors can't seem to do anything for him."

She swallowed past the lump that had formed in her throat. Searching her mind for something to assuage Conrad's fears, she gripped him tighter. Tears trickled down her cheeks and soaked his flannel shirt.

Conrad's sobbing abated, and Noreen pulled away. She squared her shoulders then pulled up his chin with her finger and gazed into his red-rimmed eyes. "Your father would not want us to grieve this way. He is going to meet his Savior. He will no longer suffer from the pain in his lungs. Here on earth, he has to fight for every breath he takes. It won't be like that in heaven." *You are tearing my heart out, Lord. Do You know that? What good could possibly come from this? A boy needs his father.* She shuddered. *And I need my husband.*

Lips trembling, Conrad nodded.

"Conrad, supper is ready. Come, eat." Edmund's mother shouted at them from the bottom of the stairs. Her gruff voice grated in Noreen's ears.

Noreen kissed Conrad's cheek, then jerked her head toward the door. "Go. She will only get louder if you don't join her."

"But I'm not hungry."

"I know, but you must make an effort for her. She is also grieving. After all, she is going to lose her only son."

Conrad trudged from the room, his footsteps fading as he descended the stairs.

Noreen spun on her heel and hastened to the bedside. She studied Edmund's ashen face. It was a wonder he hadn't awakened at the sound of their voices. Lowering herself to the chair she cradled his hand in hers and laid her head next to his on the pillow.

***

Noreen awoke with a start. She lifted her head and looked around the room. The house was silent, and darkness had fallen outside the window. The rain no longer beat against the window. Next to the bed, the lamp gave off a tentative glow.

"I love you."

Her gaze shot to Edmund's face. His sapphire-colored eyes were open and clouded with pain. She released his hand and put her fingers to his mouth. "Don't try to talk. It will only tire you."

He shook his head. "I'm running. . .out of time. . .There are things. . .say to you. You must. . .listen."

She caressed his face, willing her fingers to remember every contour. Her chest ached, and her eyelids prickled with unshed tears. Unable to speak, she nodded.

"I haven't been much. . .of a husband. . .to you. And I'm. . .sorry for. . .that."

She opened her mouth to speak, but he shook his head. "Let me. . .finish. I love you. . . more than life. . .itself. And I know you. . .love me, but you must. . .remarry."

"No. Never." Noreen set her mouth in a thin line.

"I know God has plans. . .for you. He will take care. . .of you. Have faith, *Schatzi*. Watch over. . .our boys."

Tears tumbled down her cheeks. He was always the strong one, the faithful one. Not her.

Edmund squeezed her hand in a vise-like grip and moaned.

Then his breathing ceased.

He was gone.

Noreen laid her head on his chest and wept.

Berlin, Germany, 1933

Chapter Three

The newspaper crackled as Noreen folded and tossed it on the kitchen table. The pink light of dawn filtered through the window as she drained the last of her tepid tea. Heavy footsteps sounded on the stairs. Setting the cup into the saucer with a faint clink, she turned toward the noise. Moments later Manfred entered the cozy room and dropped into one of the wooden ladder-back chairs.

He pointed to the paper and scowled. "I thought we agreed not to start our day with bad news."

Patting his arm, she tilted her head. "And a good morning to you, too."

"Sorry, *Mutti*." Fifteen year-old Manfred ran his work-roughened hand through his hair then scratched at the stubble on his cheek. "It was a long night. Conrad suffered from nightmares again. It's only been in the last couple of hours that he has been sleeping peacefully."

"The dream where he is at *Vati's* funeral?"

"Ja." He sighed. "Conrad feels things deeply. I don't know if he will ever get over *Vati's* death."

Noreen rubbed at the floral pattern on the saucer. "There are some days I feel the same way. Your father was the love of my life."

He leaned over and hugged her. "He was a wonderful father. I wish the doctors had been able to save him, but his lungs were too far gone when we moved here."

"It was not meant to be." She pinned a smile on her face. "Enough melancholy. It is Saturday. What are planning to do with your day off from school and work?"

"There is much to be done in the garden if we expect it to provide for us over the winter."

Noreen squeezed his shoulder. "Listen to you sounding like a man. You must do something fun, something that feeds your soul."

"Working in the soil does feed my soul." He grinned. "My belly, too. And that is most important."

She swatted his arm and rose. Filling the sink with soapy water she began to wash the dishes. "Speaking of your belly, there are pancakes warming in the oven. Help yourself."

"Thank you, *Mutti*. I don't know what I'd do without you."

"Make your own breakfast, I suppose."

Manfred snorted a laugh and retrieved the food from the oven before returning to his chair. He forked one of the pancakes onto his plate then sprinkled it with sugar and squeezed a lemon over the crepe-like delicacy before rolling it up. He opened the newspaper and dropped his fork with a clatter. "It's as we feared. Hitler has been named Chancellor. We're in for it now."

Noreen shrugged. "We can't be sure of that. Hitler has done some good things for Germany."

"He has visions of greatness." Manfred shook his head. "He is wily, and he has a mighty ego-a dangerous combination. You mark my words. There will be a war before he is finished."

She whirled and glared at her son. "How can you say that? What do you know of war?"

"I know it killed my father." His face darkened. "Not with a bullet, but it killed him all the same. And I hear men talking. On the bus. In the grocer's."

"What do they say?"

"That Hitler won't stop until Germany regains the respect of Europe." He poked a bite of pancake into his mouth and chewed. After swallowing, he said, "Have you read his book *Mein Kampf*? My Struggle."

"I know what it means. I can speak the language." She frowned. "Not as well as you and Conrad, but I get by."

"So? Have you read it?"

"I see no reason to."

"Too many people would agree with you." Manfred stabbed at the pancake on his plate. "But when this is all over, more people will wish they had read it. I, for one, think it's a harbinger of what's to come."

Berlin, Germany 1936

Chapter Four

"I wish your father could see you. He would be so proud." Noreen blinked away the moisture in her eyes. "You have grown to be men of great character. Strong and full of integrity. Your brides-to-be treat me with love and respect. You have chosen well." She brushed a piece of lint from Manfred's sleeve. "And you both look so handsome in your new gray suits.

Eighteen-year-old Manfred pulled her into an embrace. He tucked her head under his chin. "I miss him, too."

Conrad frowned. "Sometimes I can't remember what he looked like. Is that bad, *Mutti*?"

Noreen reached for her other son. "No, you were only seven when he died."

"I don't remember his face either, but I can still hear his voice. Deep and firm, at least until the end. He could barely speak at that point." Manfred released Noreen and turned toward his brother. "You sound like him, Conrad."

"And you both resemble him," Noreen said. "Manfred, you have his nose and jet black hair. Conrad, you are tall like he was, with his broad shoulders." A sheen of moisture obscured her view of her sons. "He may be gone, but he lives in our hearts, doesn't he?"

Music from the church sanctuary seeped into the small room where the trio waited for the double wedding to begin. A knock on the door sounded before it opened. The boys' best friend, Johann Biedermeyer, poked his head into the room. "It's time to escort you down the aisle, Frau Hirsch."

"I'll be there straight away. First, I want to pray with my sons."

"Ja, I'll be right outside."

The door closed with a quiet thump. Noreen linked her arms with the twins and bowed her head. "Dear Heavenly Father, thank You for today. Even though it is a bittersweet day because we wish Edmund was with us, we are joyful for this new chapter in the boys' lives. Thank You for Rosa and Odelia who love my sons. Please bless their marriages. Draw them closer to You. We love You and praise You for all You do. In Jesus' name, amen."

"Amen." Conrad and Manfred murmured in unison.

Noreen stood on her toes and kissed Manfred's cheek, then Conrad's. "I love you." She walked to the door and slipped outside. Tucking her hand in the crook of Johann's elbow, she straightened her shoulders. "I'm ready. Let's get these boys of mine married. Then maybe we can find you a nice girl."

As they walked through the hallway toward the narthex, Johann grinned, and his blue eyes shone. "Don't tell anyone, Frau Hirsch, but I already found a *fraulein*."

She gave him a sidelong glance. "Why the secret, Johann? You shouldn't be ashamed of her."

"That's not it." He reddened. "She is young. We must wait until her parents think she is old enough to be courted. Meanwhile, I do things for the family. Help out. And I get to see her. I am content with that."

"Martina Schmidt? Is that your sweetheart?" Noreen chuckled and squeezed his arm. "Good for you. You have chosen well."

Johann's color deepened to the roots of his blond hair. "Shhh! You can't tell anyone."

Noreen made a zipping motion across her lips. "I won't say a word. But I will pray for you both."

"From your mouth to God's ears. If he listens to anyone, it would be you, Frau Hirsch."

"Shame on you, Johann. He listens to anyone who calls on his name."

"He doesn't seem to be listening to me."

"Sometimes it is we who don't listen. He might be saying to wait. Or no." Noreen squinted over her glasses at the young man. "Look at me. I prayed that Edmund would get well, but God took him. It was a long time before I realized he healed my husband by taking him to heaven where he is no longer suffering." She sniffled. "I miss him desperately, but I will see him again. And when I do, it will be for eternity. God doesn't always give us the answer we expect."

She patted his arm. "Enough lecturing. I am pleased you have a young lady. And I am very happy to be at my sons' wedding. God is good!"

***

Berlin, Germany 1939

Noreen sat on the porch knitting with Rosa and Odelia. The orange fire from the setting sun glinted off the windowpanes. The autumn breeze lifted her hair, the graying strands tickling her face. She glanced at her daughters-in-law. "We'll go out tomorrow to collect willow branches so I can teach you to make baskets. We've talked about the craft often during these three years you've been married to my boys, but it never seems to happen."

Rosa stood and turned on the porch light. "It can't be helped, *Mutti* Hirsch. There is always some chore to do. Even now, there are vegetables to be canned."

Odelia wrinkled her nose. "I am thankful for the break. If I look at one more cabbage leaf, I'll run screaming from the house." She flushed. "I'm sorry, *Mutti* Hirsch. I shouldn't complain. There were years you and your family barely had enough to eat."

Noreen pulled a length from the red ball of yarn at her side then laid the unfinished scarf in her lap. "Those were long, hard times, but God saw us through. I know you didn't mean anything by what you said." She lowered her voice and winked at Odelia. "Besides, I agree with you. I, too, am quite tired of cabbage."

Odelia giggled. "We're like the Israelites who complained about the manna. They had plenty, but wanted something different, didn't they?"

"Yes, and God gave them quail. Should we pray for some quail, girls?"

Rosa giggled and sat down. "We could. Or we could send our men out hunting."

"That wouldn't work. Your Conrad is too soft-hearted to kill." Odelia said.

"True enough, but Manfred is the same. He just covers it up with his bluff and blather."

Noreen glanced at the oblong, silver watch-face pinned to her sweater. "Speaking of the boys, they should be home from the railyard by now. I wonder what's keeping them."

Rosa's smile froze. "Could there have been an incident? Hitler's Brown Shirts have been busy the last few nights."

"They've been focusing on the Jews. Surely with Conrad's Aryan appearance, our husbands would be left alone."

Rosa crossed her arms. "We've made it no secret we disagree with their methods. The Brauns aren't Jewish, and you saw what happened to them. Mr. Braun was flogged, and their son, Wilhem, was taken. No one knows where he is."

Noreen tucked her knitting into the bag at her feet. She stared at the blackening sky. "Germany is struggling, girls. We must pray for the country's leaders. The Treaty at Versailles left many people bitter and disillusioned. And inflation is so very high. A wheelbarrow of Deutschmarks will barely by a loaf of bread. Many think Hitler has the answer to making Germany a great nation once again."

"Except for his persecution of the Jewish people."

"And others. Hitler targets anyone he doesn't think measures up to his standards. Martina Biedermeyer told me about a group of Romany gypsies who were beaten up and arrested." Rosa shook her head. "What did they do to deserve such treatment?"

Odelia gestured to the couple sauntering past on the sidewalk. "Hush! Do you want to be overheard?"

From down the street footsteps clattered, and the three women peered toward the sound. Johann Biedermeyer emerged from the murky darkness. His face was streaked with sweat and dirt, his blue railroad uniform torn in several places. Pain radiated from his eyes as he met Noreen's gaze.

Lips trembling, he said, "There's been an accident."

Berlin, Germany, 1940

Chapter Five

Noreen laid down her fork then wiped her mouth with the linen napkin. She pushed away her empty plate. Empty. Just like her heart. A year had passed since that awful day when the boys were killed at the railroad yard while coupling two train cars. *Please God, help me understand why You took away my family.*

She shook her head to rid the gruesome vision from her mind, then folded her hands and cleared her throat. How would her daughters-in-law react to her announcement?

Odelia looked up from her plate, still partially filled with sauerbraten, its tangy fragrance hanging over the table. "What is it, *Mutti*?"

"I've come to a decision." She took a deep breath. "I hope you'll understand. I've prayed about this for a long time."

Rosa's forehead wrinkled. Her eyes filled with tears. "You're leaving Germany, aren't you?"

"Yes. I think it's best. Manfred was right when he said Hitler would bring the country to war. I didn't see it at the time." She shook her head. "I told him he was foolish to say such a thing. It's me who was foolish."

Rosa reached over and patted Noreen's arm, her calloused fingers warm against Noreen's skin. "Don't say that. You are a wise woman. Wise in the ways of God."

"You are a sweet girl. And that is why you should stay in Germany and meet a nice boy you can marry, who will provide for you. And Odelia. You are both too young to remain widowed."

"Why did you not remarry, *Mutti* Noreen?" Rosa asked.

"No man ever measured up to my Edmund." Noreen sighed, then pasted a grin on her face. "He was the only one who would have me."

Rosa snickered. "That can't possibly be true. Surely you had your pick of suitors."

"No, but that's kind of you to say."

Odelia scowled. "We're getting off the subject. Are you leaving immediately? If so, there is much to do in preparation before we go."

"We?" Noreen cocked her head. "I'm returning to England. You're staying here."

"I will go with you. Someone has to help you."

"I may be old, but I'm not infirm, Odelia. Thank you for your offer, but I will be making the journey alone."

Rosa stood and put her dishes in the sink with a thump. "No, we are both going with you. It's what family does for one another. Your in-laws took you in when you needed help, and now we are going to help you." She looked at Odelia. "You are right. There is much to be done. I will notify the landlord and secure provisions. Can you make the arrangements to sell what we won't be taking?"

The dishes clattered as Noreen cleared the table. "There is no need for you to accompany me. I'm English. Soon it won't be safe for me to stay here. You are German. You can remain with no worries."

Taking the plates from Noreen, Rosa set them on the counter. She grasped Noreen's hands. "We want to do this for you. You have loved and supported us since we first met you. We three women are alone. Let us be alone together. Please."

Odelia nodded. "Please, *Mutti*."

Noreen studied the two young women. Rosa-small and lithe, her corn-silk blonde hair wrapped in two braids around her head as a crown. Bright blue eyes sparkled above a pert nose. Even dressed in worn-out clothing, she carried a regal bearing. Odelia towered over Noreen and Rosa. She wore her dark hair pulled into a bun at the nape of her neck. Dark eyes and heavy eyebrows contrasted with her light complexion. The girls seemed to be holding their breath, waiting for her decision.

"All right. You may join me, but if you find that dreary, old England is not for you, I will understand."

Rosa squealed and clapped her hands. Odelia's face lit up.

"Do you think we can be ready in two weeks? I'd rather not delay."

"The sooner the better." Odelia hugged her arms around her middle. "Herr Hitler is not to be trusted."

***

The platform vibrated beneath Noreen's feet as the train rumbled into Berlin Station. Hordes of people shoved their way toward the iron behemoth. Babies wailed. Parents barked orders at their children to stay close. The smell of unwashed bodies mixed with the coal dust in the air.

Perspiration trickled down Noreen's face, and she scraped a damp strand of hair behind her ear. The satchel on her back threatened to tumble to the ground, so she hitched her shoulder to settle luggage back into place. The bulging bag that had traveled with her from London to Berlin so many years ago would now make the return trip.

She gripped her bulky, brown suitcase tighter and braced herself against the tide of humanity. Not ready to get swept into the train, she hunched closer to the wall. Odelia and Rosa stood sentry at her side.

Noreen glanced at Odelia's face, whiter than usual. As the departure day approached, the young woman had become quiet and withdrawn. More than once this morning, Noreen found her frozen in place, lips moving in silent prayer. When questioned, her daughter-in-law claimed she was simply petitioning for safe travel.

The loudspeaker crackled with static.

The mob quieted. A child cried out then fell silent.

"*Achtung!* There will be a slight delay due to mechanical difficulties."

A moan rose from the crowd.

"Please move back from the train. We will announce when it is time to board. Thank you for your cooperation."

"I can't do this." Odelia sobbed into her crumpled handkerchief. "I'm sorry, *Mutti.* Don't hate me, but I cannot go with you to England. I'm not brave enough."

Noreen pulled Odelia into her arms. "Hush, child. I could never hate you. You have to do what is right for you. You should stay and make your life here."

Several people stared at the trio as the young woman continued to cry. Rosa stroked her sister-in-law's back. "Where will you go? Your family is gone."

Odelia sniffed and wiped her face with the damp cloth. "I have a second cousin who lives in Hamburg. After Manfred died, she said she would take me in." She patted her handbag. "I received a letter from her last week renewing the invitation. She owns a dress shop and said I could work with her doing alterations."

Noreen opened her bag and reached inside. She withdrew several Deutschmarks and thrust them into Odelia's palm. "You will need these until you receive your first paycheck."

"No, I've taken enough from you."

"Nonsense. I insist you take them. And before you leave the station be sure to get your ticket refunded."

Rosa unwrapped the blue scarf from around her neck. She draped it across Odelia's shoulders. "It's not much, but it will keep you warm during cold nights."

Odelia's lip trembled. "Thank you. I will miss you both."

The women clung to each other while Noreen prayed.

"Your attention, please. We will now begin boarding the train to Brussels. Please proceed in an orderly fashion."

The buzz of voices filled the station as the people jostled each other. Odelia gave Noreen and Rosa a gentle push forward. "Go. Don't miss your train. I'll be fine." She held up a scrap of paper then handed it to Noreen. "This is my cousin's address. You can write to me there. We'll stay in touch."

Noreen stuffed the paper into her purse and nodded. She brushed Odelia's damp cheek. "Blessings on you, child." She turned to Rosa. "This is your chance. You can remain in Germany, too. I don't have another son or a brother who can marry you."

Rosa shook her head. "Please, don't try convincing me to leave you. If you're going, I will go, too. If you stayed, I would stay. You are my family, and even your God has become mine."

England, several days later

Chapter Six

"Next station South Croydon! Next station South Croydon!"

Despite her exhaustion, Noreen grinned at the conductor's announcement. She was home. As anticipated, the journey had been grueling. She and Rosa had changed trains in Brussels and Paris then taken the ferry from Calais to Dover. Another train took them from Dover to London where they boarded the Tube. Rosa seemed to take in everything with child-like delight.

Noreen squeezed Rosa's hand. "I am so pleased you came with me. You are going to love England."

"I will love any seat that is not moving." Rosa stretched and massaged her neck. "When we get to your, ah...*wohnung...haus*?

"Flat. Initially, we'll live in a flat. A house within a house."

"Ah, flat. Yes, well, I will lie down for at least a day without getting up."

"You say that now, but I know you. You will clean the flat from top to bottom, even though it is probably in tip-top shape."

Rosa giggled. "I can dream about a day of leisure before I try to find a job, can't I?"

Noreen chuckled. "I've thought about that. You might not be able to get a job until your papers are in order. You're a German citizen. I don't know what we have to do to get permission for you to work."

"I didn't think about that." Rosa bit her lip. "Will they send me back? I want to stay here with you."

"Everything will work out. God is with us. I've been thinking about how we can earn money. I made a good living many years ago making and selling baskets. In fact, that's how I met Edmund." Noreen swallowed the lump in her throat. Crying wouldn't help anything. "I used to weave beautiful baskets." She held out her arthritic hands. "And despite appearances, these fingers can still weave. There are many shops owners who might be willing to carry our pieces for us. And there are festivals and fairs where we can sell the items ourselves."

Rosa sagged against the seat. "I like that idea. We can be together. I'm not sure my English is good enough for a real job yet." She sighed. "And they might not like me."

Noreen shot a look at Rosa. "What do you mean, not like you?"

"I am German. Your people must not like the Germans."

"Ridiculous. Besides, anyone who doesn't like you isn't worth our time." Noreen crossed her arms and huffed.

The train bumped to a stop. "South Croydon. This is South Croydon station. All out for South Croydon!"

***

One month later

The coins clinked as Noreen dropped them one by one into her purse.

Rosa packed the unsold baskets. She glanced at Noreen, her eyebrows drawn together. "We sold fewer than we did yesterday."

"Yes, but God will provide. He always does." She jiggled the small bag. "There is enough to buy food for tonight and tomorrow. We need to be content with that."

"You are so brave, *Mutti*. I worry every night when I am lying in bed. I pray, but God is not listening to me."

"No, I'm not brave, child. I say what I do to reassure myself. I must remember God provided for my family and me during the famine in Russia, and he will provide for us now. We don't know how, but he will."

"That's the hard part. The not knowing."

Noreen tucked her graying hair behind her ear. "That's where faith comes in. Like the Israelites, we must step out in faith, knowing God will do something wonderful for us."

Rosa shook her head and resumed packing. She snickered. "Maybe the people on the bus will buy our baskets so we will stop dragging them onboard and taking up so much room."

"We can only hope!"

"Noreen Wilson, is that you?"

Noreen's gaze shot toward the voice. She hadn't heard that name in nearly thirty years. A rotund woman with blonde hair styled in a victory roll rushed across the grassy expanse of the village green. She waved her black leather purse and clamped her hand on the wide-brimmed, straw hat perched on her head. A bucktooth grin lit up her face.

"Noreen Wilson, I'd know that face anywhere. When did you return to England? The last I heard you were married and living in Russia of all places. How could you possibly stand all that cold? Is this your daughter? She's beautiful. What's in the boxes?"

The woman took a breath, and Noreen grinned. Kathryn Bramwell. It had to be. No one else chattered like she did. "Kathryn Bramwell?"

The woman put a hand to her chest. "It's Kathryn Howarth now. Been married for the last twenty years." She gestured toward her wide hips. "And he doesn't seem to mind the extra pounds."

Noreen hugged her friend. "My surname is Hirsch now. It's wonderful to see you. Where do you live? Do *you* have children?"

Nodding, Kathryn dug into her handbag and extracted an envelope. She withdrew several pictures that she held up to Noreen. Three girls and a boy. I'm praising God my son is only eleven. Too young to be called up." She looked with interest at Rosa.

Noreen gasped. "I'm sorry. Where are my manners? Kathryn, this is my daughter-in-law, Rosa. Rosa, this is Kathryn Howarth. We attended secondary school together."

Rosa dipped her head. "How do you do?"

Kathryn's eyebrow lifted. "You're German?"

"*Ja*, but I have no family there, so I came to England."

"What about your husband, Noreen's son?

Noreen's throat tightened. "He's gone. I have. . .had. . .two sons. Manfred and Conrad. They were killed in a train accident. And my husband, Edmund, he died too. Gas from the Great War. He was never the same when he came back."

"Oh, how awful for you. Of course you returned to Croydon. It's important to be with one's own people." Kathryn peered at Rosa. "How do you like England, dear?"

"*Es ist wunderschön. . .*ah. . .wonderful. Everyone has been so kind."

Kathryn cocked her head, and her dark eyes flashed. Noreen was reminded of the goldfinch that used to live outside her bedroom window.

The town hall clock chimed, and Noreen looked at her watch. "Goodness, we must get these baskets home. There are chores to do before night falls. It delightful to see you again, Kathryn."

"Those boxes are filled with your baskets? You always created such gorgeous work." Her gaze pierced Noreen's eyes. "Are you in financial difficulties? Is that why you're here on the green? To sell your baskets?"

Noreen's stiffened. Now everyone would know she was poor. "Well-"

"I have been unable to find work." Rosa nibbled her lower lip. "As you said, I'm German. My papers seem to be taking a long time to. . .what is the word. . .be final."

"Your working papers haven't been approved yet?" Kathryn thrust out her chin. "How ridiculous. We shall take care of that, won't we? My Peter is in the Ministry of Labor. You'll have your permit in no time." She rummaged in her handbag and pulled out a pencil and tiny notepad. She scribbled on the top sheet and tore it off. "Here's the address for Peter's office. I will speak with him tonight. You visit him tomorrow, and he'll take care of everything."

"How can you say that?" Noreen frowned. "We've been trying for weeks."

Kathryn squeezed Noreen's arm. "Unfortunately, the people you've been dealing with are little cogs in a big machine. My Peter runs the machine. It's all in who you know."

Rosa curtsied. "You are most kind."

"Aren't you sweet? It's what friends do for each other. Now, what sort of skills do you have? Do you type? Have you ever done office work?"

"*Nein*, er. . .no. I kept house and worked in our garden. We grew our own food."

"Excellent. You're a perfect candidate for the Land Army. They're always looking for girls to work Basil Quincey's fields." She winked at Rosa. "Perhaps you can teach them a thing or two."

"Land Army? I don't want to carry a gun."

Kathryn guffawed then covered her mouth for a moment. "I'm sorry. How rude of me. It's not that kind of an army, dearie. You would work at one of the farms planting and harvesting produce."

"I would get paid to work in a garden?"

"Yes, my dear, you would. The biggest garden you've ever seen."

Rosa clapped her hands and grinned. "I would like that very much."

A light breeze lifted Noreen's hair, and she glanced at the sky. *Is that you, Heavenly Father? Once again, You have provided for us in a way we never expected. You've sheltered us, and now You've provided food. I don't deserve Your grace. My heart cries out in awe and gratitude.*

Kathryn tucked her bag under her arm. "I must be going. Lots to do. I'm so glad I ran into you. Don't forget. Stop by to see Peter first thing in the morning." She waggled her fingers and rushed down the sidewalk. "I'll tell him to expect you."

Noreen and Rosa exchanged a glance then burst out laughing.

"She always was a formidable force." Noreen said. "Hard to say no to, I would imagine."

"God answered your prayer, didn't he? You prayed, and he sent her to you."

"To us. God is taking care of both of us, Rosa. And yes, he did answer my prayer." She frowned. "We'll see about you working on this Basil Quincey's farm. The only Basil I remember was a cruel and dishonest man."

Chapter Seven

Noreen sat at the kitchen table, her dog-eared Bible open in her lap. She glanced at her watch, and her stomach clenched. Rosa had been gone for six hours. She insisted she could make the journey to the Ministry of Labor on her own. Would Kathryn's husband come through as she had promised? Did he have the authority to grant Rosa her working papers?

"Forgive my doubts, Father. As usual I'm running ahead of you and worrying about how things will turn out. Thank you for providing the money we need to purchase food. And thank you for sending Kathryn to us. Help me believe her husband is the answer to our prayers."

Peace settled over Noreen, and she rubbed her eyes. "Thank You, God."

She rose from her seat and set the iron kettle on the stove. While she waited for the water to boil, she stared out the window. Nestled among the branches of the nearby elm tree, a robin fed her chicks. They wriggled and bumped each other, mouths gaping. For several minutes the mama bird dropped food into their open beaks.

A shrill whistle filled the air. Noreen turned off the gas and lifted the kettle off the burner. Pouring the hot water over the tea leaves in the strainer, she sighed. "You keep reminding me, don't you, Lord? After all this time of being provided for, you would think I wouldn't stumble with doubt and discouragement. But I'm tired. So very tired. And lonely. Why did you have to take Edmund? Why couldn't you heal him here on earth? It's not fair. You took my entire family, Father. What sort of plan includes that?"

Tears trickled down her cheeks. She swiped at them with stiff, aching fingers. Holding out her hands, she examined her swollen knuckles. England's damp weather exacerbated her arthritis which made weaving more difficult than usual.

She squared her shoulders. If Rosa could work in the fields, Noreen could endure the pain of making baskets.

A key sounded in the lock. Noreen yanked a towel off the rack by the sink and wiped her face. She tossed the cloth on the counter and pinned a smile on her face before turning toward the door.

Rosa burst in with a wide grin. Wisps of hair had escaped from the pins holding down her blonde tresses and framed her flushed face. She slipped off her coat and hung it on a hook by the door. She opened her handbag and held up a sheaf of papers. "It's official. I am allowed to work in England!"

Noreen clapped her hands. Rosa rushed forward and smothered her in a hug. "I'm sorry it took so long, but after I got my papers, I went to the Land Army office to sign up. I've been assigned to Mr. Quincey's farm. Mrs. Howarth must have spoken with them. Everything was arranged before I got there."

A chill swept over Noreen. Who was this Basil Quincey? Was it the same man she remembered who derided women and participated in shady businesses? "Come, child. Sit down. I was just about to have a cup of tea. Join me."

"*Ja*. That would be good. It's a bit *kühl* outside."

Noreen prepared a second cup of tea, and the women sat down at the table.

Rosa wrapped her hands around the warm vessel and sipped the steaming amber liquid. "Mmmm. It is warming me up from the inside." She glanced at Noreen, and her smile turned to a frown. She set the cup down with a thunk then grasped Noreen's hands in hers. "Here I am talking all about me while you are upset. You have been crying. What's wrong?"

Pulling away Noreen gave a dismissive wave. "It's nothing. Just a bit of melancholy this morning. It happens. I want to talk about you. Tell me everything. It will go a long way to making me feel better." She took another sip from her tepid tea. "Please. Tell me."

"If you insist." Rosa cocked her head and squinted at Noreen. "But I'm worried about you."

"I'll be fine."

After a long look, Rosa pushed away her tea and spread the papers on the table. She smoothed out the creases then pointed to the signature at the bottom. "As you can see, it's official. I was quite nervous, but I prayed to God, and he gave me a sense of calm." She sat back in the chair. "You have taught me well to lean on God."

At least one of us isn't full of doubts, Lord. Noreen patted Rosa's hand. "Good for you. What is Mr. Howarth like? I have a hard time imagining who would marry Kathryn." She grinned. "He must be a man of few words."

Rosa nodded, and her bell-like laughter filled the kitchen. "You're right. He asked very few questions. He wanted to know about my experience working in the fields. He said I looked too frail for farm work, but I assured him I was up to the task. I told him about our gardens at home. He seemed satisfied after that. He mumbled something about his wife's projects. Apparently, he thinks I may be one of them."

"But what does he look like?"

"He's a big bear of a man. Even sitting behind the desk he looked quite large. His blond hair is cut very short, giving him a military appearance. But he had friendly-looking brown eyes." She shook her head. "But he also seemed weary. There were stacks and stacks of papers on his desk. He must work a tremendous number of hours."

Noreen rubbed a scratch on the wooden table. "What did he say about your assignment? Does he know this Mr. Quincey? It could be dangerous to work for a man you don't know."

"He spoke highly of the man. Said Mr. Quincey has changed a great deal in the ten years since his father passed away and he inherited the farm. In fact, Mr. Howarth said Mr. Quincey is a Christian. No one believed him at first." Rosa blushed. "Apparently, he was a bit of a *Schurke*. . .uh. . .scoundrel as a young man."

"Scoundrel is right. He had no respect for authority, and treated women as if they were only created to do his bidding. He spent lots of time at the pubs, and it wasn't just for the food." Noreen clenched her fists, and the nails on her hand bit into her palms. This Quincey fellow *was* the man she knew. Only God could have changed a man like that.

Rosa's gaze shot to Noreen's face. "You know him?"

"Yes, more than I'd like to admit. He's a distant cousin. Five or six times removed. But his behaviors make me ashamed to be related."

"Why didn't you say anything when Mrs. Howarth mentioned him? Was he that bad?"

Massaging her knuckles Noreen looked past Rosa out the window. How much should she say?

"*Mutti?*"

"Most of what I know is third-hand." Noreen rubbed her forehead with a cold hand. "I cannot abide gossip, but it's important you know what was said about Mr. Quincey."

Rosa sat back and crossed her arms. "None of that matters. He's different now. A Christian. God has wiped away his past sins."

"True, but you are best served by entering into this with your eyes open."

"If you insist on telling me, I will listen. But you must give Mr. Quincey the benefit of the doubt. The woman in line behind me was assigned to work his farm, too. She said he has done many charitable things in the community."

Noreen raised an eyebrow. "Interesting. In the past he was driven by the accumulation of money. His father's farm was successful, but Basil always wanted it to be more. Bigger. More profitable. There was a drought, and many farms failed. In desperation, the owners had to sell. He was the only one buying, and he paid less than market value." She swallowed. "And it didn't matter if the owners were related to him."

Rosa's eyes widened. "He did your family wrong, didn't he?"

"Yes." Noreen failed to keep the bitterness from her voice. "He waited until we were nearly starving when he approached my father. Said he could make his credit problems disappear." She shivered. "But he insisted that I be part of the bargain."

"How so?" Rosa's voice was barely above a whisper.

"He said he would only purchase the farm at my father's asking price, if I became his courtesan. Who even uses that word?" Noreen snorted. "When my father asked why he wouldn't marry me, Basil said he wouldn't marry outside his class." She sighed. "Fortunately my father refused the offer. But he was never able to sell, and eventually the bank took possession. Basil was able to pick up the property for a fraction of its worth."

Rosa's hand clutched at her throat. "How awful. You must hate him."

Noreen shook her head. "Not anymore. Edmund helped me see how useless it was to hold on to the anger. Basil was a ruthless man. Is a bit of money scattered here and there toward worthy causes enough to prove he has a new heart? Has God changed him? Is he a new man? Frankly, that remains to be seen."

Chapter Eight

"You must work faster, Rosa. Mr. Quincey expects this field to be planted by dark."

"I'm sorry, Allison. I've worked in gardens all my life. I didn't think it would be this difficult." Rosa waved her arm across the landscape. "It's so overwhelming. I can't see the end of Mr. Quincey's fields."

She brushed her tangled hair away from her face with a calloused hand then stretched. Needles of pain shot through the muscles in her lower back. Two weeks plugging potato eyes, and she still couldn't keep up. The other workers were nice enough, but she saw the criticism in their eyes. Her slow pace meant they had to work harder. And longer.

"Your problem is you look up too often. Focus on the ground. Dig the hole. Poke the potato chunk into the ground. Cover it up. Move on. It's that simple." The lanky woman three rows away gestured with her spade to the rich, brown dirt. "You're a dreamer. This is an easy job, but you can't be thinking about other things."

Working two rows past Allison, Marla Kearson guffawed. "If the stupid German woman hasn't figured out how to plant potatoes in the two weeks she's been here, nothing you say is going to help."

Several of the other land girls chuckled, and Rosa's face burned. Heart pounding, she gripped the trowel and plunged it into the ground. Marla was getting bolder with her mean-spirited barbs.

Allison tossed a clod of dirt toward Marla. "Mind your business, Kearson. If memory serves, you did quite a bit of whining when you first arrived."

Marla scowled and bent to shove a potato chunk into the hole.

Rosa sat back on her heels. "Thanks for sticking by me," she whispered. "I won't let you down."

"It's not me you have to worry about." Allison White jerked her head toward the top of the ridge where a lone man sat astride a huge, black stallion. "It's him."

Rosa glanced at the rider, and a chill swept over her. His wide-brimmed fedora was pulled low on his face, but she'd bet money that Mr. Quincey was staring at her. She tugged at the ill-fitting Land Army uniform then rolled her eyes. What was she doing? She was a hired farmhand. And not a very good one. How long before het let her go?

***

Basil shifted in the saddle. The leather creaked and groaned under his weight. He reached forward and patted Major's muscular, ebony neck. The horse nickered softly and bobbed his head.

"Anxious to move on, old boy? You'll have to wait. I want to see how Mrs. Hirsch fares." He chuckled to himself. Now I'm discussing my business with a horse, albeit a magnificent Arabian. Shrugging, he continued. "Who is this delicate woman assigned to the Land Army? They must be desperate for workers."

The sky blazed with purple and pink as the sun sank toward the trees. Basil looked at his watch then gazed at the laborers scattered amidst the furrows of dirt. Primarily wives and widows from the surrounding villages, with a few single girls shipped in from London. Mrs. Hirsch's slender figure was an anomaly among the stocky, handkerchief-headed women.

Shaking his head, he sighed. He should have released her after the first week. She worked hard, but was always the last to finish. There were quotas to meet. The government wouldn't accept excuses.

But she was a widow, one of many. And the Bible commanded to look after them, and that's what he meant to do. With or without the Crown's permission.

Hoofbeats approached. Basil waited until the rider pulled alongside him before he turned.

"This was delivered by messenger. I thought you'd want to see it straightaway." Sixty- five-year-old James Sullivan extended a slim, buff-colored envelope toward Basil. A veteran of the Second Boer War, James had lost an arm in the Battle of Bergendel, but that hadn't stopped him from saving his platoon before passing out from loss of blood.

He had returned to the farm upon his release from the hospital and worked harder than two men. Father had quickly promoted him to foreman, and Basil saw no reason to change that after his father's death.

James cleared his throat. "How goes the harvest?"

Basil studied the man's face. "As you can see, the field is not as finished as it should be. "Slow, but steady. But you already know that. Is this your way of telling me we need to sack Mrs. Hirsh?"

James's face reddened. "She's holding back Mrs. White. The woman slows to the young Mrs. Hirsh's pace, probably so she won't be lonely. But that doesn't get the work done."

Rotating his neck to ease the stiffness from his shoulders, Basil frowned. "Then we should hire additional hands. There must be others who need a job. God has blessed me with an exceptional amount of money. If I can't use it to help the less fortunate, what good is it?"

James scowled. "We've a business to run, not a charity. Your father would be disappointed at the change in you."

Basil's chest tightened. "Then so be it." He narrowed his eyes at the foreman. "If you're concerned about your wages, perhaps you should seek employment elsewhere."

"That. . .that's not it." James stammered. "The government inspectors will be here any day now, and they'll want to know why we're behind schedule."

"And we'll tell them the truth. We have new workers who are not yet up to scratch. Then we'll remind them it's my money that's paying these people. If they have a problem with that, they can send more laborers at their expense. After all, I'm doing them a favor by picking up the tab."

"Yes, sir." James shook his head and continued to frown.

Basil knotted the reins in his hands. Was he being irresponsible with the business by giving Mrs. Hirsch some leeway? Should he let her go and hire a replacement? How long would it take for a new worker take to perform as required?

Major whinnied, and Basil loosened his grip on the leather straps. "Sorry, old man. Didn't mean to yank on the bridle." He glanced at James. "Be honest with me. How do the others feel about Mrs. Hirsch? Do they think I'm being unfair by allowing her to continue with us?"

James heaved a loud sigh. "Actually, they're as barking mad as you are. They don't seem to care that she lags behind. They say she learned the technique quickly enough, but she struggles to keep the pace. She tires easily." He jerked his head in Rosa's direction. "She's not exactly built for farm work. The others indicate she is friendly, and they like her, so are willing to overlook her deficiencies."

"Then I'll overlook them, too, for the time being."

"Doesn't it bother you that she's not one of us?"

Basil raised an eyebrow.

James licked his lips. "Mr. Quincey? You do know she's German, right? How could the Ministry of Labor hire her?"

"Yes, I'm aware of her ancestry. But she's German, not Nazi. There is a difference. If the authorities aren't bothered by her heritage, then neither am I." He curled his lip. "And you shouldn't be either. Is that clear?"

"Whatever you say, Mr. Quincey." James hauled on the reins of his horse. The animal wheeled around and thundered back toward the barn.

Basil shrugged. James would have to live with the decision to keep Mrs. Hirsch. It wasn't money out of *his* pocket. Did he care so much about the government inspector? That wasn't his concern either. And he certainly shouldn't worry about where Mrs. Hirsch came from.

Laughter floated toward him from the field. He glanced at the trio of women plunging their shovels into the rich soil. They grinned at each other then continued to make their way down the furrow.

Rosa stretched and swiped a dirt-encrusted hand across her forehead knocking her hat askew. She tugged it back into place. The setting sun silhouetted her slim form. His heartbeat quickened. She was like a delicate orchid. Slender and exquisite. Unlike any woman he had ever met.

She looked in his direction, her face still wreathed in joy. His cheeks warmed, and he yanked his fedora lower on his forehead. He'd been caught staring like a schoolboy. What must she think of him?

Chapter Nine

"The selection gets worse by the day. Even if you have ration stamps, there's nothing worth purchasing."

Rosa eyed the woman standing on the other side of the bin that held five mottled potatoes. She poked one of the mealy-looking tubers and nodded. These were definitely not from Basil's farm.

She nibbled the inside of her lip. When had she begun to think of him as Basil instead of Mr. Quincey? It had been three weeks since he sat on his horse and stared at her from the top of the hill. He visited all of his fields each day. Why should she think he had a special interest in her?

Tucking two of the lesser-bruised potatoes into her canvas bag, Rosa moved to the bread display. It was so much cheaper to make bread, but by the time she got home from work, there were not enough hours left in the day to bake. And Noreen would never admit her hands were getting worse. Weaving was hard enough, she shouldn't be expected to knead dough.

Her mother-in-law never complained, but her pain was evident. New lines had appeared on her face, and she massaged her knuckles when she thought Rosa wasn't paying attention.

Rosa walked to the shelves stacked with tinned goods. She grimaced. Her friends in Germany would never believe she ate canned food. She could barely believe it herself. Basil was generous with his workers, allowing them to take less-than-perfect produce home. He also gave them more than enough bread and cheese for the mid-day meal, apparently intending for the employees to pocket the extra food. But there was a limit to what he could give them.

She hummed Beethoven's *Moonlight Sonata* and swayed to the music while she perused the shelves. Last week Basil had given her extra green beans. When Allison had asked her to hold her bag while she donned her jumper, Rosa felt the difference in weight. Was that when he went from Mr. Quincey to Basil?

Rosa whispered to herself. "Basil." The name hovered on her lips. "Basil."

"Excuse me?" An elderly woman with crimped gray hair and round wire spectacles stared at her. "Were you speaking to me?"

Shaking her head, Rosa dropped her gaze. She'd been caught mooning over her employer. Without looking at the labels, she tucked several tins into her bag.

"Are you alright, dear?"

"*Ja.* I mean yes."

The woman drew back, and she gasped. "You're German. What are you doing here?" She lunged at Rosa's bag. "You don't deserve the right to shop here. You should go back where you came from."

Rosa clutched her satchel. "But-"

"Nothing you say will make any difference." The irate customer stalked past Rosa, holding her handbag close as if she would be contaminated by an unintentional touch. She disappeared around the rack of government pamphlets, but her shrill voice carried throughout the shop. "Mr. Devereaux, are you aware you have a Nazi in your establishment? I'm not sure I care to do business with a sympathizer."

Rosa's shoulders slumped, and she dropped her bag with a thud. Wrapping her arms around her middle, she fought to keep from crying. Didn't the woman understand that Rosa wasn't a Nazi, that she hated them, too? She was German and wanted Germany to be a proud nation again, but not to the detriment of the Jews or the others Hitler was exterminating.

She bent and picked up her bag. Slinging it over her arm, she peeked around the display of booklets to see if the horrible woman had left the store. Swallowing past the lump in her throat, Rosa blew out a deep breath. She'd have to find another market again. The grocer shouldn't be penalized for being nice to her. It wasn't the first time a customer had objected to her presence. When would she remember to keep her mouth closed? Her eyes flooded. Perhaps it was time to take Noreen up on her offer to do the shopping.

***

The bus bucked and shimmied as it rumbled over the macadam street. The acrid smell of petrol filled the crowded vehicle. Voices rose and fell. Periodic laughter cut through the buzz of conversations.

Rosa gripped the canvas shopping bag in her lap and studied the floor. If she didn't meet anyone's eyes, she wouldn't be expected to speak. The bus turned a corner, and a small pebble rattled down the aisle. The vehicle made another turn, and the stone rolled back where it started.

Tears formed in her eyes, and her lower lip trembled. *I'm just like that rock. Pushed by forces I cannot see. And it will only get worse as the war continues and Hitler gets more aggressive. Maybe I shouldn't have followed Mutti Noreen to England. Is she in danger because of me?*

Digging into her purse, Rosa found her handkerchief. Crying was useless. She must be strong for her mother-in-law. Noreen needed her. At least until Rosa could save enough money to leave her in comfort.

Who was she kidding? At her wages, the two of them barely had what they needed to make ends meet. There was rarely any left over.

"Are you all right, missy?" The woman next to Rosa patted her arm.

Rosa nodded. She would not be lured into talking, no matter what the woman said.

"Are you sure?"

Nodding again, Rosa shifted in her seat and turned her face toward the window. Perhaps that would stop the busybody.

"I'm Mrs. Winslow. I have a daughter about your age. Her husband has been called up. Perhaps that's why you are upset? Is your husband gone too?"

Still mute, Rosa shook her head and continued to peer out the window at the passing shops. How far until her stop? Maybe she should get off at the next one and catch another bus. Rudeness went against every fiber of Rosa's being, but she couldn't let anyone hear her accent.

"She's not going to talk to you, Louise, so you may as well leave her be." A buxom, dark-haired woman wearing a WACs uniform sat across the aisle.

"I'm just trying to help."

The brunette shook her head. "She's got all the help she needs. Don't you know who she is?"

Rosa cringed when her seatmate shook her head. Did the woman think she was deaf?

"Noreen Hirsch's daughter-in-law. You remember Noreen. She went to London after secondary school then married some *German*. They left England, and then she came back without him a few months ago. I heard she was widowed. Serves her right."

Mrs. Winslow leaned over and hissed at her friend. "German? Does that mean-?"

"Yes. This girl is German, too."

"Why haven't the authorities sent her back there?" Mrs. Winslow tossed a look over her shoulder at Rosa then drew her skirts closer. She dropped her voice to a whisper. "She could be a spy."

First the woman in the shop, and now these two. Would she ever be trusted in England? A moment later the bus lumbered to a halt, and Rosa sprang to her feet. "Excuse me." She pushed past Mrs. Winslow and stumbled into the aisle. Hurrying toward the door, she avoided the looks of the other passengers.

The door remained closed. Rosa turned to the driver who scowled at her. "You're a Jerry? If I'd a known that, you never woulda got on my bus. You're never going to be safe. We're going to kill every one of you."

Chapter Ten

Misty fog enveloped Rosa as she trudged down the gravel road toward Basil's farm. Mutti Noreen must not discover she walked to work since the incident on the bus with Mrs. Winslow last week. Fortunately, her mother-in-law hadn't seemed to notice Rosa left earlier than usual today.

She pulled her scarf over the bottom of her face to block the chilly, morning air. Shivering, she wrapped her arms around herself and increased her pace. The muffled roar of an engine approached. She stepped into the grass and waited for the vehicle to pass. The bus's shrill horn was followed by the blare of the driver's voice. "Get out of the way, you no-good Jerry. Go home!"

Rosa's chest tightened. She fought the urge to run. Words couldn't hurt her.

The noise faded.

Silence descended.

Moments passed. Rosa peered at her watch. If she didn't hurry, she would be late. She broke into a jog, and her legs ate up the distance to the farm. Cold nipped at cheeks. Her ears ached.

The twin boxwoods at the entrance to Basil's farm came into view. She slowed to a brisk walk then wiped the perspiration from her upper lip. Straightening her jacket, she stiffened her spine and marched through the gate. She strode toward the barn to pick up her bushel baskets and the day's assignment.

None of the dozen or so women milling about in the cavernous building glanced her way as she entered. Good. For once, perhaps she blended in.

Bales of hay were stacked in the far corner, their earthy aroma filling the space. A pair of broad-shouldered oxen stood strapped to a large, wooden wagon filled with stacks of empty baskets. The animals snorted, their breath coming out in white puffs. They stomped their hooved feet, apparently anxious to get going.

Rosa joined the queue to collect her baskets. The hair on the back of her neck tingled. Was someone watching her? She surveyed the group and gasped. Marla fixed a malevolent glare in her direction. Rosa shivered and dropped her gaze.

"Good morning, ladies! Thank you for coming today."

Rosa whipped her head around at the sound of Basil's voice.

***

Basil cleared his throat. "I am pleased with the amount of work you have completed thus far this season. Some of you have never done this type of job prior to coming here. You are to be commended for your efforts."

His gaze raked the crowd. Where was Rosa? He spied her in the back of the crowd. She seemed to be studying her feet. Was something wrong? Was she injured? She looked up and smiled. His heart skipped a beat, and time seemed to freeze.

Sullivan coughed. "You all right, Mr. Quincey?"

Basil glanced at his foreman. "Yes. Yes. Ah. . .sorry. Where was I?"

"You were going to announce the dinner."

"Of course." Basil turned back to the women. He focused his eyes on the far wall of the barn. That would be less risky than watching Rosa. Rosa, whose fair complexion had deepened to a golden tan after weeks of fieldwork. Whose blue eyes sparkled even when the sun wasn't shining in them. Rosa, whose—

"Mr. Quincey?"

Basil shook his head. Sullivan must think he had lost his mind. "Right. As most of you are aware, the field in the north end of the farm is the last to be planted. All of you will be working there today which means it should be finished by noon or thereabouts. In recognition of your accomplishments, I will be serving a full meal with more than enough to ensure you have plenty to take home."

The women applauded, and their faces glowed.

He held up his hands until the noise abated. "I'm also giving you one week's paid break. You deserve some time off to spend with your families."

Murmurs rose. Basil raised his voice. "I expect you back here in seven days. Bright and early, and ready to get back to business."

"Thank you, Mr. Quincey." Allison White shouted from her position next to Rosa. "Three cheers for Mr. Quincey."

"Hip, hip, hooray! Hip, hip, hooray! Hip, hip, hooray!"

Basil shuffled his feet in the dirt and waved his hand.

Sullivan clapped his hands. "All right, ladies. Enough celebratin'. Let's get to work."

***

Rosa strolled along the table spread high with food. Even after all her co-workers had been through the line, there was still enough to feed a small army. She speared a succulent-looking piece of ham and laid it on her plate. After filling the remainder of her plate with green beans, she popped one of the tender spears into her mouth.

She turned and searched the grounds for Allison. With the exception of Marla and her friends, the other workers spoke to Rosa, but Allison went out of her way to be pleasant and sociable. She was the only one who didn't seem to mind Rosa came from Germany.

Allison waved at her from beneath a large elm tree. Rosa stopped to pick up a cup of apple cider before joining her friend. She sat down on the blanket Allison had spread out then propped her back against the wide trunk. She took a deep drink and set the cup between a tangle of roots protruding from the ground. "Can you believe this meal?"

"There are definite benefits to working as a Land Army girl. We'd be scrimping in London." Allison poked a carrot chunk into her mouth. "I've never had such delicious vegetables in all my life."

"In Germany-"

Allison scrambled to her feet, plate in hand. "I just remembered I have something to do."

"What? Where are you going?" Rosa looked past Allison, and her heart skipped a beat. Basil was walking toward them.

"See you later." Allison grinned and trotted toward the barn.

Rosa glared at Allison, and her friend's giggle floated in her direction.

Basil stopped in front of her. "I hope I'm not disturbing you, Mrs. Hirsch. I only wished to see if you are getting enough to eat." He shoved his hands into his pants pocket. "Mrs. Talbot has packed up boxes of food for each of you to take home. Be sure to take yours."

"Yes, sir. You have been very generous despite my inability to keep up with the others." She lined up the beans on her plate, then set the dinnerware on her lap. "I deserve to be sacked, you know."

"You'll get the hang of it." He shrugged and gestured to the ground. "Do you mind if I join you. I don't wish for you to have to crane your neck to speak with me."

Rosa's heart beat faster, and she licked her dry lips. "Please."

"Thank you." He settled himself next to her and stretched out his legs. His shoulders brushed hers, and she clamped her mouth shut against the gasp that threatened to spill out.

His faced reddened.

Rosa took a sip of cider to hide her smile. He was apparently as nervous as she was.

"How are you getting along, Rosa, uh, Mrs. Hirsh? Do you enjoy the work?"

"I'm fine." She drew in a deep breath then let it out with a whoosh. "I love to be outside, especially working in the dirt. Gardening is such a miracle. One buries the seed, and with a bit of water, sunshine, and time, a plant is born. It burrows through the soil to reach the surface seeking sustenance and light."

Basil stared at her, and she ducked her head. He must think her a ninny. Spouting off about miracles.

"I'm sorry. I do go on."

"There's nothing for which to apologize. Your point is well stated. Although I must admit I never thought about farming as being a miracle."

"I didn't either in the beginning. But then *Mutti* Hirsch introduced me to her God. I see the miracles he provides every day. We must work the ground, but he rewards our diligence. Even in times of want."

"You are a Christian?"

Rosa swallowed. Would he be offended by her answer? "*Ja.* I mean yes. I accepted Christ as my Savior shortly before Conrad and I married."

"That's wonderful!" Basil's face lit up. "I'm a Christian, too. I came to God as a child."

Rosa wilted against the tree and bowed her head. *Thank You, God for providing yet again. This time with a boss who is a Christian.* She cocked her head. "That is why you are so good to us, isn't it? You are taking care of the 'least of these,' aren't you?"

He nodded. "Yes. God has blessed me with riches beyond compare. I am compelled to share them. Other businessmen think my actions are foolish."

"You must answer to God. Not to men."

"Exactly! You understand." He squeezed her hand then drew back as if burned.

She nibbled her lower lip. Her hand tingled where he had touched her. Did he feel that too?

***

Sullivan reached for another box in the stack and handed it to the last worker in line.

"James, a moment, please."

He looked up to see Mr. Quincey jogging toward him. James beamed at the brunette woman and touched the brim of his hat. "Good day, madam."

She dipped her head and hurried from the building.

James turned toward Basil. "Sir?"

"Have you given Mrs. Hirsch her allotment yet?"

"No."

"I'd like you to add half again to her box. Understood?"

"But, Mr. Quincey, that's not fair to the others."

Basil frowned. "I don't remember asking for your opinion."

"No, you didn't. But sometimes you need to hear it."

"Just do what you're told." Basil spun on his heel and strode out the door.

James scowled. What was the boss thinking? Mrs. Hirsch was a German. A Jerry. Probably a Nazi. She didn't deserve extra portions even if her mother-in-law was English.

He pulled off his hat and raked his fingers across his closely-shorn hair. It was this kind of playing nice behavior that Lord Chamberlin had tried with Hitler. "And we see how well that worked. We're at war with them."

Clamping his hat back on his head, he grabbed the top two boxes of food and set them on the ground. He popped open the flaps and dumped the contents of one into the other. *In for a penny, in for a pound.*

"Mr. Sullivan?"

James whirled at the sound of the voice. Mrs. Hirsch stood near the pyramid of cartons. How long had she been there? Had she heard him?

"Aye? What can I do for you?"

"I'm, uh, here for my allotment of leftovers."

"Good timing. I was just preparing yours." He bent and lifted the carton. He handed it to her and said, "'It's a bit heavy, but you should be able to manage. There's a bit extra in it for you and your mother-in-law."

Her eyes widened. "That's very generous of you, Mr. Sullivan. We're grateful for your help."

"Think nothing of it." He forced a smile to his face. Maybe if she thought he was interested in her, she'd give up some of those German secrets. Time would tell.

Chapter Eleven

Rosa trudged up the steps to the house then set the heavy box on the porch with a thump. Her arms throbbed, and her fingers ached from gripping the carton for so many miles. As she reached into her purse to dig for her house keys, the door flew open.

"You're home." Noreen's forehead was wrinkled into a frown. "It's late, even for you. Is everything alright?"

"I'm sorry to worry you, *Mutti*." Rosa pushed her sweaty bangs away from her eyes. "We finished in the fields around one o'clock then Mr. Quincey provided a celebration meal. I stayed to chat with Allison White. She has been very nice to me."

"I remember you telling me about her. Her husband is in the RAF, yes?"

Tapping the box with her foot, Rosa nodded. "We received extra food at the farm today. As grateful as I am, it took longer to get home with it than I expected." She stretched her arms.

"Didn't you take the bus? It's not that far to the house from the bus stop."

Rosa bent and hefted the container into her arms. What could she say to Noreen without telling an outright lie? "Let's get the food into the ice box. We don't want it to spoil."

Noreen pushed the door wider and stepped aside. "Of course! I'm sorry. I shouldn't have left you standing on the front stoop. How thoughtless of me."

"Nonsense. You could never be thoughtless."

They tromped through the hall to the kitchen where Rosa plunked the box down on the table. She sighed and dropped her pocketbook into one of the chairs before tucking her bedraggled hair behind her ears. She opened the box and busied herself with putting away the produce. "I could use a bath and a lie-down."

Noreen wrapped her arm around Rosa's shoulder and guided her to the nearest chair. "First, a cup of tea."

"But-"

"No arguing. I will finish putting away the food. You rest." She filled the kettle with water then set it on the stove and lit the gas. Humming quietly, she emptied the box and stored the items.

The kettle shrieked, and Rosa rubbed her forehead. Would her mother-in-law forget about her question regarding the bus?

Minutes passed as Noreen went to the stove and readied their tea, the soft clink of china filling the kitchen. When the tea finished steeping, she placed the teapot in the middle of the table then set Rosa's cup in front of her. She lowered herself into the chair, cup and saucer in her hand. She sniffed the aromatic liquid. "Nothing like a good cup of tea to smooth away the day's troubles and worries. Don't you agree?"

"I still prefer my *kaffee*, but yes, I enjoy your English tea." Rosa took an exaggerated slurp. "You do make a good cup."

A faraway look entered her mother-in-law's eyes. "Edmund also liked my tea. I combine several kinds of leaves. It's better with sugar, but we've run out of this week's ration." She wrapped her fingers around the dainty cup. "I should share my secret recipe, so you'll have it when I'm gone."

Rosa's gaze shot to Noreen's face. "What are you saying? Are you ill?"

Noreen set down the cup. "No, but I'm not getting any younger. And don't forget, this is war. We must be realistic. Hitler has increased the number of bombings. It could just be a matter of time. . ."

"Don't talk like that." Rosa gripped Noreen's arm. "Won't God keep us safe?"

"We don't know God's plans, dear. He took Edmund and my boys. He could choose to take one or both of us home. To be honest, I'm ready to go. I'm tired of struggling, and I miss Edmund desperately."

"From what you've told me, it seems he loved you very much."

Noreen drained the last of her tea. "Enough. Reminiscing makes me maudlin, and we have much to be thankful for." She gestured to the empty carton. "A box was packed full of food, for one thing. How can Mr. Quincey afford to give so much to each employee?"

"Actually, I think I got a bit more than the others."

"Really?" Noreen narrowed her eyes at Rosa. "How do you know that?"

"Mr. Sullivan told me. When I entered the distribution area, he said he was filling our box, and that he included extra for us. Wasn't that nice of him? I thought he didn't like me. He's usually a bit. . .what is the word. . .*knapp*."

"Terse? James Sullivan is that way with everyone. It's my guess that he doesn't like having a passel of women on his farm."

"But it's not his farm, is it? He works for Mr. Quincey just like I do."

Noreen poured more tea into her cup. "True, but he's worked there since Mr. Quincey was a lad. Maybe before he was born. That gives him a sense of ownership."

"Does he know you? Why would he give me additional food for you?"

"His son, Harry, went to school with me. We stepped out together for a while. I think he hoped we would marry."

"Then you met Edmund."

"No, Harry and I broke it off long before that. He was a nice enough chap, but we had very little in common."

"So, it's not me that Mr. Sullivan cares about. It's you!"

"I doubt that. Besides, he was probably acting on orders from Mr. Quincey. James Sullivan may feel like he owns the farm, but he doesn't. And the extra food isn't his to give away." Noreen grinned. "With any luck, you have caught Mr. Quincey's eye."

Rosa dropped her gaze and studied the dregs of her tea.

"Aha! That's it, isn't it? You and Mr. Quincey have taken a shine to one another. If Basil is truly a new man, the Christian you say he is, this could work to our favor."

"*Mutti* Hirsch, don't say it like that. Besides, he is a rich land baron. I am but a poor immigrant. It wouldn't be right for us to. . .be together." The memory of Basil's touch came to mind, and she shivered.

"As a rich man, he can do whatever he likes. But even if he doesn't marry you, he may be willing to help us. He's a distant cousin of mine. Maybe there is some responsibility there. I wonder if there are any laws that compel him to provide support." Noreen rubbed her forehead. "To be honest, I'm struggling to forgive Basil, but if he is one of God's children, he might be the answer to our prayers."

Rosa stared into her cup. "He is already, as you say, helping us. He gave me a job I don't deserve. He gives me food to bring home. We can't expect more than that."

"We'll see." Noreen stood and cleared the table. "Enough talk. You should go rest, and I need to get back to my weaving. In all the excitement about your provisions, I forgot to tell you my news. I sold all but three of my baskets today."

"How exciting! I'm not that tired. I can help you. We can make twice as many for you to sell tomorrow." And maybe the weaving would take her mind off a certain handsome land owner.

Chapter Twelve

Two weeks later, Rosa and Allison entered the barn in the late afternoon. Rosa eyed the enormous, brown and white cows hitched to the wall. One of them bellowed, and she froze. "Maybe this isn't a good idea, after all."

Allison pushed her toward the behemoths. "Nonsense. You said you wanted to learn how to do other things around the farm. Milking is an important job. You're a smart girl. It won't be long before you're milking with the best of us."

"They're so big and. . .smelly. But mostly big."

Her friend's musical laughter echoed in the cavernous building. "Everything on this farm stinks in one way or another. Be glad you're not learning to feed the pigs. Now, that's an odoriferous job." Allison pinched her nose and made an exaggerate shudder.

Rosa giggled. "You and your vocabulary words. Bet you never thought you'd have a use for that one."

Allison laughed and grabbed a pair of stools from the corner. She jerked her head toward a stack of buckets. "Get you a couple of those and follow me."

The women approached the closest cow, and Allison dropped the stools next to the animal with a clunk. She patted the bovine's rump then took one of the buckets from Rosa and set it beneath the udder. She lowered herself onto the seat. "Put aside the other bucket and sit down."

Rosa's gaze jumped from the snuffling, snorting nose of the cow to the trifling, three-legged stool. "The pigs aren't as big."

"No, but they can get mean, or at the very least, aggressive. Trust me when I tell you, this is the job you want. Now, stop being such a scaredy-cat. You started a brand new life in a strange country. If you can do that, you can learn to milk a cow."

***

Pffft. Pffft. The milk hit the aluminum bucket in a rhythmic stream.

Rosa rotated her shoulders and shifted on the stool. Allison was right. She could learn to milk a cow. Not nearly as efficient as her friend, she had managed to finish three of the beasts without too much trouble. Now for a momentary break to flex her aching fingers.

"Moooo." The animal rolled a large, brown eye toward Rosa.

"Sorry, girl." Rosa rubbed the cow's flank. "Guess I got over confident."

"So, now you're talking to the cows. That's not good."

Rosa's head whipped around. Basil smirked as he strode toward her. Her palms slicked with moisture. That wouldn't help her milking capabilities. She clamored to her feet. The stool fell on its side with a clatter, and she bent to retrieve it. He reached for it at the same time, and their hands met on the wooden leg.

Her fingers tingled, and she heard his quick intake of breath. She released the stool and tucked a stray hair underneath her hat. "Just passing time, Mr. Quincey."

"No harm, Rosa, er, Mrs. Hirsch. These girls like a bit of conversation." He stroked the cow's forehead.

Allison appeared behind Basil. She carried a pail in each hand. "I'll be back. I'm taking these over to Flo. She's filling the canisters for shipping."

"I'll bring this one." Rosa pointed to the milk-filled bucket under the cow.

"Don't waste a trip. Wait until you've finished a second one." She tipped her head at Basil. "I won't be but a few minutes." She marched out of the building, whistling Tommy Dorsey's tune *This is No Dream.*

"I didn't mean to interrupt your work." Basil shoved his hands into his pockets and rocked back on his heels. "I wanted to see how you fared with your first milking experience. Seems you're doing fine."

"Allison is a good teacher." Rosa laid her hand on the cow's back. "And your animals are cooperative and patient."

Basil chuckled.

Rosa nibbled her lower lip. Was he laughing at her? He was older by a good bit. Did he think her a foolish child because of her excitement at this simple farm task? He had been performing these chores most of his life. No doubt he could do them in his sleep. She grabbed the pail from under the cow and set it by a bale of hay, then picked up an empty bucket.

"Do you like working here?" Basil's eyebrows were drawn together. "You never complain, and it's arduous labor. How do you feel about that?"

"I'm not one to shy away from hard work. And it's not much different than my garden." She gripped the handle, the cool metal bit into her hand. "Well, it's slightly bigger than my little vegetable plot, but I'd much rather be outside digging in the soil than doing anything else. Besides, I'm not brave enough to work in the munitions factories like other girls."

He leaned toward her. "Don't shortchange yourself. You're one of the most courageous women I've ever met."

Dropping to the stool, she began to milk the next cow. "That's nice of you to say."

His voice hardened. "It's the truth. Think about it. You left your home to take care of your mother-in-law in a country where you barely knew the language. I'm not sure I could do that."

"You're angry."

"I could never be upset with you." He blew out a breath. "And I may be overstepping my bounds when I say this, but I get frustrated at how you belittle yourself. You are a beautiful woman, full of kindness and integrity. You have a strength of character that I haven't witnessed in a long time." His face reddened, and he crossed his arms.

"Mr. Quincey!"

Basil whirled. Victor, the thirteen-year-old son of his housekeeper, sprinted toward him. "Mr. Sullivan says to come straight away. It's a UXB."

Basil tossed a glance at Rosa, his face ashen. "Where?"

"In the west field."

"Mrs. Hirsch, stay here. I've got to go." He and Victor raced from the barn.

Rosa stared at the empty doorway, her heart pounding. What was a UXB?

She sighed and turned back to the cow. Did he really think she was beautiful?

***

"Evacuate the workers from that end of the property." Basil trotted next to the young man, his breath coming in gasps.

"Yes, sir. Mr. Sullivan saw to that. He said for you to call in the discovery of the unexploded bomb, since you were nearer to the telephone. He's waiting for you near the site."

"Not too close, I trust."

The boy shrugged. "I'm to notify the rest of the workers."

Pain knifed his side as Basil ran into the house. At fifty-four, he was getting too old to be running at breakneck speed. Lifting the receiver, he waited for the familiar voice of Gertrude Parks, the local operator.

"Number please."

Basil rattled off the information, his voice coming in ragged bursts.

"Just a moment, sir."

A series of clicks sounded, then ringing.

"Home Guard. Sergeant Irving speaking."

"Sergeant, this is Basil Quincey of Dorset Farm. One of my men has just discovered an unexploded bomb in one of my fields. Please notify the authorities."

"Right away, sir."

Basil hung up the phone with a bang then sank into the wooden chair against the wall. He scrubbed at his face with cold hands. So close to death, yet the UXB was found. Closing his eyes, he prayed, "Thank you, God, for protecting me and my employees. Your goodness knows no bounds." With a deep sigh, he opened his eyes and headed out of the house. There was no time to waste.

Rosa's face came to mind. He told her she was beautiful. Shaking his head, he frowned. She must think him an old fool for saying such a thing.

Two weeks later

Chapter Thirteen

A knock sounded at the bedroom door.

"Rosa! Mr. Jenkins is here." Noreen's voice was muffled.

"Be right there." Rosa finished brushing her hair then inspected her reflection in the mirror. The robin's egg blue dress was one of her older garments, long out of style, but in good condition. Her shoulder-length, blonde hair shone despite the dim lighting in the bedroom. Conrad always said it was her best feature.

Her chest tightened. Was she being unfaithful to her husband's memory? They had agreed that if anything ever happened to either one of them, the other should remarry. But that discussion had occurred when they were young and arrogant enough to believe they would live forever.

Then he died.

And she came to a country where falling bombs killed innocent people every day.

The unexploded bomb discovered at Basil's farm had been a close call. Rosa shuddered. Would she survive the war? Would any of them?

Tonight's outing was one date, not a marriage proposal. Mr. Jenkins was nice enough. He sought her out at church each week to speak with her. And he didn't seem to mind she was German. That alone gave him a leg up. He was a Christian and had a good job as a butcher. She turned away from the mirror and picked up her handbag.

She shook her head. She wasn't looking for a husband, and it was just as well. Suitors weren't exactly beating a path to her house. They probably never would.

But she was tired of being lonely. The other girls went out. Why shouldn't she? Mr. Jenkins had asked to take her to the cinema to see the Judy Garland/Mickey Rooney comedy *Babes in Arms*. It would be fun to do something other than darning socks or listening to war reports on the wireless.

"Buck up, Rosa. You can do this."

***

Two weeks later, Rosa gazed at the clear, starlit sky as she and Mr. Jenkins sauntered along the sidewalk. It was the third time he had taken her out. He whistled the Benny Goodman song the band played as their last number at the dance.

She wiggled her toes. They hadn't ached this badly since she and Conrad had danced all night at their wedding. Sighing, she blinked away the tears that threatened to run down her cheeks. She cleared her throat. "Thank you for escorting me tonight, Mr. Jenkins. I had a wonderful time."

"Martin."

"What?"

"Call me Martin. It's my name. Mr. Jenkins is my father."

Rosa raised her eyebrows. "That's rather forward, wouldn't you say?"

"Perhaps before the war, yes. With times so uncertain now, no." They stopped at the bottom of the steps of the home where Rosa's flat was located. He turned her toward him and held her hands. "Of all people, you know how short life can be. I like you. A lot. Would you consider allowing me to court you?"

"I, uh. . ." Rosa moistened her dry lips. Her heart beat faster. Should she let him court her? Was it time to put away the memories of her life with Conrad? Mr. Jenkins was kind, but did she love him? Could she love him?

Noreen would say she should try.

Mr. Jenkins squeezed her fingers. "It seems I've rendered you speechless. Is it because you are overwhelmed with love for me?" He leaned toward her and chuckled. "I can barely see your face in the blackout. Are you terrified at the thought?"

"Not terrified. This is all very sudden. I didn't realize you had feelings for me." She gently extricated her hands from his and crossed her arms.

"Why do you think I asked you out?" He tilted his head. "Is there someone else?"

Basil's face came to Rosa's mind, and she closed her eyes against the vision, but it wouldn't disappear. His crystal-blue eyes twinkling and mouth set in a crooked grin when he teased her about milking "the girls," as he called the cows. His strong, tanned hands grasping the reins of his giant, black stallion. His rumbling laugh that rang out across the fields when he was carrying on with the men.

Rosa nibbled her lower lip. Was there someone else? No. Basil could never marry her. Did he want to? Just because he was gracious to her, didn't mean he was in love with her. Besides, he was from the upper class. A wealthy land owner. She was poor, not even earning enough money to put food on the table and pay the rent. Noreen had to sell baskets to add to Rosa's salary. More importantly, Rosa was German.

Basil could never marry a German.

Mr. Jenkins kissed her lightly on her forehead. "I can see you need time to get used to the idea. How about if we talk about this next Saturday? If the weather cooperates, we could go on a picnic."

"That would be lovely. Thank you." Rosa gestured toward the house. "It's late. *Mutti* Noreen will be worried."

"Yes. Of course." He bowed and touched the brim of his hat. "Sleep well, Rosa."

She nodded and hurried up the steps. Jamming her key in the slot, she unlocked the door and slipped into the house. She shut the door and leaned against it, glad for the unlit room. Tears slid from her eyes.

"Conrad, why did you have to leave me?"

"Rosa, what's wrong?" Noreen's voice pierced the darkness.

Chapter Fourteen

The following day, Noreen glanced at the watch pinned to her sweater. Only three minutes later than the last time she looked. She picked up a towel and dried her hands, massaging her swollen knuckles with the threadbare, brown cloth.

Tossing the towel on the floor next to the bucket of willow branches, she sat back and studied the basket on the table in front of her. The upright stakes were a warm shade of umber. The weavers were from a blackberry bush she found on the way home from the market. The contrasting colors of the two materials presented a pleasing combination. Hopefully, one of the housewives who frequented her table would agree.

She rotated her neck to ease the stiffness from her shoulders. Time to prepare the tea.

Anne Lenner's clear soprano voice sang from the wireless. So much better than the harsh tones of some of the American singers. Noreen hummed as she rose and made her way into the kitchen. She put the kettle on the stove and turned on the gas. While the water heated, she arranged tea cups and saucers on the carved wooden tray she had traded for one of her baskets. It had been a good deal. Brian Collander charged a lot for his items.

A knock sounded at the front door.

Noreen froze. Was she overstepping her bounds with what she was about to do?

She smoothed her hair and squared her shoulders before striding through the house. Taking a deep breath, she opened the door.

Basil stood on the porch, hat in hand. He dipped his head. "Good morning, Mrs. Hirsch. I hope I'm not too early. For once the Tube ran without delays."

Noreen gawked at him. "You take public transportation, Mr. Quincey?"

"Yes, madam. No need to use petrol rations unnecessarily."

Basil rode the Tube, gave his workers extra food, and contributed money to myriad causes associated with the war. How could she reconcile that with the man who had degraded her and practically stolen her family home? She shook her head and stepped aside. This was about Rosa. Noreen's hurts needed to be shelved, at least for the moment. "Please, pardon my manners. Won't you come in?"

He entered the house, and she viewed the sparse living room with his eyes-the worn chairs, the faded blue couch with the unfortunate sag in the middle cushion, the scarred end table. Why had she invited him here?

"If you'll have a seat, I'll be back straightaway with the tea."

"Why don't I join you in the kitchen? That will make things easier for you, yes?" He seemed to search her face. "Unless you'd rather serve in here."

Was he embarrassed by the evident poverty in her home? She pinned a smile on her face. "The kitchen is fine." They walked to the back of the house, and she gestured to the ladder-back chair near the window.

He moved to the corner of the kitchen and picked up the unfinished basket. Tilting it back and forth, he studied it for a long moment. "I heard you were an expert weaver, but this piece is exceptional. I appreciate how you've blended the colors of the wood."

Her grip tightened on the tray as she carried it to the table then poured tea into the delicate china cups. "Thank you. I'm not sure how much longer I can continue. The arthritis in my hands makes the work difficult."

"I'm sorry to hear that. It's obvious you get great joy from your work. Beauty springs from the passion of the artist."

He sat down and hunched his shoulders. Kneading his fingers, his gaze skittered from her face to the floor. He coughed then cleared his throat. "Before we go any further, I must apologize to you. My behavior was abhorrent when I approached your father about you those many years ago." He passed a hand across his eyes. "I'm ashamed of who I was then. An inconsiderate, arrogant pup who made an inexcusable request. Can you forgive me?"

Noreen searched his face. *Can I do this, Lord?* A sense of peace settled over her, and she sighed. With a deep breath, she laid her hand on his arm. "God has forgiven me, therefore I can do no less for you. Let's speak no more of the past."

His eyes welled, and he wiped away the moisture. "Thank you. You are a gracious woman. I don't deserve your mercy."

She reached for her teacup, and he held up his hand. "Wait. I have something for you."

He pulled a handkerchief from his shirt pocket and laid it on the table. Unfolding it with great care, he looked at her with raised eyebrows and a saucy grin. Nestled in the pristine cloth were two sugar cubes. "I have been saving these for a special occasion."

Tears sprang to her eyes, and she swallowed the lump in her throat.

His forehead furrowed. "I didn't mean to make you cry."

She swiped at her wet cheeks. "For the moment, you reminded me of my Edmund. That's the sort of unselfish gesture he would have done for me. 'Tis generous of you to share your sugar ration with me."

Basil patted her arm then reached for a spoon. Scooping up one of the tiny white squares, he dropped it into her cup with a plop before adding the second cube to his drink. He stirred the liquid for a moment then lifted the cup to his lips. Taking a sip, he sighed. "Nothing like a bit of sweetness in one's tea."

Noreen swallowed a laugh. An affluent, worldly man who could have anything he wanted. Yet, he sat in her worn kitchen and asked her forgiveness. Maybe he *had* changed, and their discussion wouldn't be as awkward as she anticipated.

She rubbed the rim of the saucer for a moment. "I appreciate you coming to see me. You're a busy, important man."

"Busy, yes. Important, no."

"Maybe not in your eyes, but the community sees you as a powerful man. Even more so than your father. From what I understand you have tripled his holdings."

"God has blessed me with a head for business."

"He has blessed you, indeed." Noreen nodded. "And I'm grateful for your willingness to hire my daughter-in-law. Not many business owners would do that. She speaks highly of the manner in which you treat your employees. The extra food you allow her to bring home has helped us tremendously."

Basil's eyes narrowed. "You're welcome. It is a pleasure to give back to the community. But I don't think you invited me here to express your gratitude. I sense you have something more to say. Now, what would you like to discuss?"

"Rosa." Noreen licked her lips, tasting the residual sweetness of the sugared tea. "I have had a full life with a wonderful man who loved me. I have no desire to marry again. My daughter-in-law is still young. She shouldn't spend her remaining days alone."

His fingers tightened on the cup. "Why are you telling me this? I'm only her employer."

"Word around town is that you appear to pay special attention to Rosa. And she told me that her most recent bag of food was heavier than that of the other girls. You're a fair and honest man. Maybe I am making a leap in logic, but I believe you may have feelings for my daughter-in-law."

"I am too old for her."

"Is that what you have been telling yourself? That's foolish. Edmund was older than me. Age doesn't matter when two people are in love."

Basil's head shot up, and he peered at Noreen. "What are you saying?"

"Rosa has feelings for you, but she refuses to acknowledge them. Her excuse is that a rich man could never marry a poor immigrant worker-a *German* immigrant. So, she tries to content herself with someone she believes is more appropriate."

"She's seeing someone? Do I know him?"

"Martin Jenkins." Noreen shrugged. "He's asked to court her."

Basil frowned. "Martin Jenkins, the butcher?"

"Yes, he attends the same church we do."

He swallowed the last of his tea then rubbed his forehead. "He's older than I am!"

"He seems to be serious about marrying Rosa." She cocked her head. "Apparently he doesn't think their age difference is an issue."

Basil leapt up from the chair and stared out the window, his back to Noreen. "You say she cares for me?"

"Yes, and you need to do something about it before you lose her."

Chapter Fifteen

Two hours later the front door slammed, and Noreen flinched. Rosa was home. She would know Noreen was hiding something. Better to get the conversation over and done with.

Footsteps sounded in the hallway then Rosa appeared in the doorway. "How was your day, *Mutti?*"

Noreen gestured to the completed basket Basil has held earlier in the day. "I created a new design. What do you think of it?"

"It's beautiful." Rosa clapped her hands and hurried to the table where the basket sat among loose twigs and Noreen's cutting tools. "You have an excellent sense of what goes together. Are those the blackberry branches you found?"

"Yes. And I have enough left over for two or three more baskets." Noreen picked up one of the boughs. "I'd like to find more of these bushes. I think their uniqueness will allow me to sell more pieces."

"You could speak to Basil, er, Mr. Quincey. He has a rather large field of them."

"Are they not all allotted to the Ministry of Food?"

"I hadn't thought of that." Rosa's brow wrinkled. "But I think a portion of his crops is for personal use."

"It's an idea." Noreen stood then washed and dried her hands at the sink before lifting the lid of the pot on the stove. "Dinner should be ready in about thirty minutes. Why don't you go upstairs and lie down for a bit? I'm sure you're tired. I can call you when the food is ready."

"I'm fine. I'd much rather have a cup of tea and visit with you."

Noreen lit the gas under the kettle. She turned toward Rosa. "You're a special woman to want to spend time with your old mother-in-law. I thank God every day for your presence."

Rosa's face reddened, and she ran her finger along a scratch on the table. "It's no more than you would do for me."

"I noticed you didn't refute my comment about being old."

Rosa's color deepened. "I'm sorry! You're not old!"

"I'm teasing you." Noreen grinned. "I shouldn't do that. You're a sweet girl." Her smile faded, and she crossed her arms. "Are you lonely, Rosa? Is that why you come straight home from work? Don't you have any friends to go out and do things with?"

"There's Mr. Jenkins."

"I mean girlfriends who you can laugh with and talk about girl things. You know, like the latest fashions or hairstyles, or any number of handsome movie stars."

Rosa shook her head. "Those subjects don't interest me. Besides, most of the girls go straight home, or the ones who are billeted on the farm go to their rooms."

"Isn't there anyone you talk with?"

She rubbed her arms as if cold. "Allison White. She's been nice to me. Seems to have gone out of her way to do so."

Noreen narrowed her eyes. "Are you telling me that none of the other women will speak to you?"

"They're busy."

"That's rubbish."

Rosa shrugged and continued to study her hands.

The kettle whistled, and Noreen sighed. She prepared two cups of tea and set them on the table. She returned to the stove and poked one of the potatoes in the soup with a fork. Shame on the other workers for avoiding Rosa. No doubt because she was German.

Pressing her lips together, Noreen ladled the steaming food into bowls and put one in front of Rosa and the other at her own place. She yanked open a drawer to retrieve silverware. She plunked the basket of fresh rolls on the table and sat down.

"You're angry." Rosa's voice was barely above a whisper.

"Yes, I'm angry. I've no time for pettiness and elitism. Those girls are working on a farm just like you. They are no better than you, nor are you better than them. Why can't they see that?"

"The women are resentful. Their husbands, brothers and sons are being killed, and their lives are being forever changed by an unwanted war. They need someone to hate, and I'm the closest target." Rosa lifted a spoonful of soup to her lips and blew on it. "They're to be pitied, really."

Noreen stared at Rosa. "You never cease to amaze me."

Rosa pinked again. "Your soup is *köstlich*. Delicious. Reminds me of the potato soup my *Großmutter* used to make."

"Changing the subject? Fine." Noreen bit off a corner of the bread. The warm, yeasty texture filled her mouth. More German words peppered her daughter-in-law's vocabulary than usual. She was upset. Had Noreen pushed the girl too hard? She swallowed and patted Rosa's shoulder. "Forgive me. I'm being a busybody."

"I'm grateful for your love." She smiled. "Because that's why you do it. Conrad told me stories about when you stood up for him. A mama tiger, and I'm glad to be one of your cubs."

Tears rushed to Noreen's eyes. "I do love you. As if you were my own daughter." She blinked and wiped her eyes with her napkin. She cleared her throat. "Which is why I have to tell you what I did."

Rosa set her spoon down and straightened. "This sounds serious."

"Mr. Quincey was here."

"What?" Rosa gaped at her.

Noreen tucked a stray hair behind her ear. "I invited him. Someone needed to intervene before you both make a terrible mistake. I told him about your Mr. Jenkins." Her words came in a rush. "About his proposal to court you, and how you think you have to accept, not because you care for him, but because you think you have no other choice."

"Why would you do that?"

"Because you care for Mr. Quincey. Dare I say it-you love him, or at least have the beginning of love in your heart for him. You don't love Mr. Jenkins."

"But I can be content with him. As you said I have no other choice."

"No, I said you *think* you have no other choice. You are a beautiful, giving woman who has too many years left to spend them alone. Especially too many to spend with someone in contentment rather than true love. You deserve to marry Mr. Quincey. He can provide for you better than any man in this town. And he does love you. Deeply."

"I cannot marry him. If you think the girls don't like me now, they would surely hate me if I married the boss. Besides, what makes you think he loves me?"

"Because he gave me every excuse he thought mattered to you. And he was horrified at the thought of your union with Martin Jenkins."

"How could you do this? Does he believe I put you up to this? What must he think of me?" Rosa hunched into herself. "I will put in a request for transfer tomorrow."

"No, you won't." Noreen held up her hand to stem the flow of Rosa's words. "Hear me out. He loves you, but he needs to know you would be open to a marriage proposal from him. He is a powerful man, but he would be dreadfully hurt if you rejected him."

Rosa shook her head. "He is a strong, confident person. He would not be hurt."

"Yes. He. Would. Even the most confident person is vulnerable when he's in love."

"You're sure he loves me?"

"Absolutely."

A look of wonder crossed Rosa's face before turning to resolve. She laced her fingers. "What do you have in mind?"

"That's my girl." Noreen drained the last of her cold tea then leaned toward her daughter-in-law. "He is having a harvest party at the end of next week. You will attend wearing your wedding cloak and-"

"Is that appropriate?"

"Yes. It is a family heirloom. You wore it to Conrad's funeral. This event is nearly as important."

"*Ja.*" A single tear slipped down Rosa's cheek.

"I know you loved my son, and he will always hold a place in your heart. But you are young. It is perfectly acceptable to love, and to marry, again. You are not being disloyal to his memory."

"I do care for Mr. Quincey." Her lower lip trembled as she smiled. "Basil."

"You will wear the cloak to the party, and when all the guests have departed ask him to retrieve your cloak. When he drapes it across your shoulders, let him know the significance of the garment. Indicate that you would give it to him if he so desires. By that act he should realize you would accept his proposal."

Rosa picked up her spoon. "Then I must finish my dinner. We have much work to do if my cloak is to be ready in time."

Chapter Sixteen

The harvest party was in full swing. Rosa stood in the corner of the barn and nursed her cider. The animals had been cleared from the building, and fresh hay scattered throughout. Couples laughed and talked as they danced to the music played by the five-piece swing band Basil had hired. Two doors propped across sawhorses were covered with cured meats and fresh, cooked vegetables. Guests walked the length of the make-shift table and heaped succulent food onto their plates.

Basil stood near the doorway chatting with Mr. Sullivan and Mrs. Pennington, the local billeting officer. The woman bent her svelte figure toward the men while giggling and tossing her hair. Widowed when her rich, older husband died after the horse he was riding failed to negotiate a jump, she seemed to be on the lookout for a replacement.

Rosa smoothed the skirt of her lapis-colored taffeta dress. The boat-necked bodice buttoned up the side and was nipped in at the waist. Obviously created before war-induced rationing, the flared skirt contained countless yards of material. A lace petticoat peeped out from underneath.

Noreen had traded numerous baskets with one of the consignment shop owners to secure the outfit. Perhaps it was a cast-off from someone like Mrs. Pennington, who wore a black, form-fitting dress enhanced by a single strand of pearls. Her shining blonde hair was swept into a chignon in which tiny flower blossoms had been tucked.

The flock of hummingbirds in Rosa's stomach launched themselves into acrobatic flight. She clenched her teeth and swallowed the lump that formed in her throat. Noreen's plan sounded so lofty when the two of them discussed it over soup and tea. She should go home and not try to compete with the likes of the wealthy widow.

No. She would see this through. It meant a lot to her mother-in-law.

Rosa straightened her spine and approached the brimming punch bowl. As she ladled some of the frothy, golden beverage into her empty glass, Marla bumped into her from behind. Liquid poured down the front of Rosa's dress and onto her freshly polished shoes.

Marla's eyes widened, and she snickered. "Oh, I'm sorry. How clumsy of me. Your dress is ruined. I guess you'll need to leave."

Kitty Underwood, Marla's sidekick tittered behind her hand. "That stain is the best thing to happen to that dress. It's entirely unsuitable."

Rosa hunched into herself, and tears sprang to her eyes. Marla had caused her to spill the drink on purpose. She'd needled Rosa ever since her arrival on the farm, but this act seemed exceptionally acrimonious.

"What do you expect from a *German*? They're barbaric." Marla spoke in a stage whisper, and a trio of nearby women gawked at them.

"I still don't understand why she's allowed to work here." Kitty tossed her head. "Do you think the authorities know about her? Perhaps we should report her."

Marla shook her head. "I'm sure Mr. Quincey has done everything by the book. He's a bit of a do-gooder. I'm sure he hired her out of pity." The pair looked down their noses at Rosa, then Marla spun on her heel, and Kitty trotted away behind her.

Rosa cringed, and her gaze searched the room for something to mop up the mess. Her face crumpled, and her eyes filled with tears. She turned and barged into Allison who appeared from nowhere.

Allison grabbed her arm. "Where are you going? I saw the whole thing and swiped one of the cloths from the floral display. Use it to swab your shoes." She gestured to the dark stain spreading down Rosa's front. "I'm afraid the punch has already soaked into your dress."

"I can't use that to clean my shoes!"

"Sure you can. And be quick about it."

Rosa pressed her lips together and shook her head.

"Fine. Then I'll do it for you." Allison knelt in the dust and wiped the sticky residue from Rosa's pumps before dabbing at her legs. "Good thing no one has any stockings, or they'd have been a mess, too."

"I can't believe you used Mr. Quincey's good linen. And you stole it!"

Allison pursed her lips. "I didn't steal it. I haven't left the premises. What else was I supposed to do? It was the closest thing available." She climbed to her feet and cocked her head as she examined Rosa. "That will have to do. Perhaps you should retrieve your cloak and cover up, make the stain less apparent."

"No! I mean, I don't trust Marla not to do it again, and I don't want anything to happen to my cloak. It's very special to me."

"Well, you certainly can't go home. That would score a victory for Marla and her ilk." Allison scowled. "She never seems to get caught by Mr. Quincey. I think if he knew her true character, he'd sack her."

Rosa sniffled and laid her hand on Allison's arm. "You're very nice to come to my rescue. I'll be fine. Mostly I'm ignored, but Marla isn't the first person to treat me like this."

"Mrs. Hirsch. Miss White. What are you doing with that cloth?" James Sullivan stomped toward them, his face dark. "The boss worked hard to spruce up the place."

"I. . . I'm sorry, Mr. Sullivan. I-" Rosa stammered.

Hands on her hips, Allison tipped her head to one shoulder then the other. "Don't get your knickers in a twist, James-old-boy. We were having a bit of a chin wag, and one of your lovely guests knocked into my friend here. Couldn't let her simply stand there and drip." Allison held out the wet material. "Feel free to do something with this. It's no longer of any use to us."

Sullivan drew back as if stung. "Show a little respect, Miss White. You don't want to find yourself permanently assigned to mucking stalls, do you?"

Allison curtsied. "Your wish is my command."

He raised an eyebrow. "Give that to one of the servants. They'll know what to do with it." He leered at Rosa. "You'd be a fit bird except for that nasty stain. How'd you manage to afford a get-up like that?"

"It was a gift from my mother-in-law. I've never had anything so beautiful."

"Word around town is that you two are poor as church mice. Sticky fingers are the only way you could get your hands on that."

"That's not true. *Mutti* Noreen traded her baskets at the consignment shop on High Street. You can ask them yourself. They'll tell you."

Allison wrapped her arm around Rosa's shoulder. "Let's take a walk, Rosa. We don't have to explain ourselves to the *foreman*. Good night, Mr. Sullivan."

"I'm warning you, Miss White. Your work could get difficult."

"Good night, Mr. Sullivan. We can discuss my performance on Monday morning. I'm currently off duty." She gave a mock salute and guided Rosa toward the barn entrance.

***

Hours later Rosa stood behind the barn staring over the moonlit field. People trickled away from the party, and Allison has departed thirty minutes ago. Soon Rosa would be the only guest remaining. Could she go through with the plan? If she did, there would be no turning back. Mr. Jenkins would know she was rejecting him. Would he be hurt? Upset?

He was a gentleman in the truest sense. Solicitous and attentive, he seemed to go out of his way to make her feel special. But she didn't love him, and *Mutti* Noreen was right. A lifetime was too long to live with a man you didn't love. Nor was entering a loveless marriage fair to him. She should have informed him before coming to the party, but it was too late now.

"Here you are." Basil's baritone voice sounded from the darkness.

She turned, her heart beating in her ears. Could he hear the thudding? She licked her dry lips. "Yes, I was enjoying the view."

He traversed the distance between them with confident strides. "You haven't had enough of looking at these fields day after day?"

"No, I could never tire of it. The dark, loamy soil. The anticipation of tiny, green shoots poking their heads into the sunlight. The plump, ripe fruits and vegetables."

"A farmer through and through." He eyed her dress. "Although you don't look the part tonight." He raked a hand through his hair. "You're lovely. That color becomes you."

She shivered. It was time.

"You're cold. I'll be right back." He returned with her cloak and wrapped it around her buttoning it at the neck. "'Tis an exquisite garment. Where did you get it?"

"It's my wedding cloak. The family heirloom is special to me, but. . ." She compelled herself to meet his gaze. "You may have it if you like."

He looked at her for along moment, his eyes unreadable in the black night. Did he understand what she was saying? Would he reject her unspoken words? Maybe she wouldn't need to turn down Mr. Jenkins.

No. She could never marry Martin. He deserved a woman who loved him with all her heart. If Basil did not want her, she would remain single.

"I will speak to Martin Jenkins."

Rosa's heart skipped a beat. "What? Why?"

"Although it pains me to say it, he has first right of refusal. I know the two of you have been walking out together. I don't want to stand in his way if he wishes to marry you."

"But what if I don't want to marry him? What if I was getting ready to break off our relationship?"

Basil's white-toothed smile flashed in the darkness. "Then you would make me the happiest man on earth." He drew her into his arms and tucked her head under his chin.

She leaned into him as the rhythm of her heart matched his.

He pulled away and peered down at her. "Go home and wait for word that I have spoken to Jenkins. It's late. I will have one of the servant lads drive you home to ensure your safety."

"But I must return to work on Monday. There are many tasks to be done now that the harvest has been completed."

Kissing her forehead then the tip of her nose, Basil shook his head. "Effective immediately your services are no longer required. And if I have my way, you'll be too busy preparing for a wedding to work my farm."

Chapter Seventeen

The sun was nearing its zenith when Basil hurried across the market square. He had been awake all night replaying the scene with Rosa in his mind. She loved him. She wanted to marry him. Now, to make that happen.

Farm business had absorbed most of the morning. Sullivan had been more cantankerous than usual, one of the plow horses had thrown a shoe, and the grain elevator had jammed. It took three men and several hours to get it operational again.

He tugged at his collar. Perspiration trickled down his back underneath his suit coat. Compared to last night's chill, the day promised to be unseasonably warm. Perhaps he was overdressed, but Jenkins needed to know it was a serious discussion.

Pushing open the door to the butcher shop, Basil eyed the jangling bell that announced his arrival.

"One moment, please!" The muffled voice came from behind the curtain that divided the store from the man's living quarters.

Basil gazed around the immaculate room. The large, service counter split the space in half. Behind it, a wooden table stood under the window, a shiny cleaver lying on top. A stack of white paper and a roll of string waited on the shelf above. A calendar was tacked to the wall to his left, black Xs marking off the days.

The curtain opened with a swish, and Martin Jenkins appeared. His dark hair was combed to one side and slicked down with oil. The white apron he wore over his light blue shirt and dark pants contained rust-colored stains.

Jenkins's face fell. "Quincey. What brings you here? Your staff has already come today for your order."

"Yes, I'm sure they have. I'm here to discuss a matter of importance. I would have come earlier, but there were several mishaps at the farm this morning."

"It's just as well. The queue winds round the building at that time of day." Jenkins yanked a towel off the rack and wiped his hands. "The women are aware that I run out early."

"Of course. I hadn't thought of that." Basil stuffed his hands into his front pockets. "Is now a good time? I could come back if you're busy."

Jenkins swept his arm across the shop. "As you can see, the shop is yours."

Basil glanced over his shoulder. "It's a private matter. Is there somewhere we could talk?"

Jenkins strode to the front door, flipped the sign, and pulled down the blind on the door. He turned toward Basil. "Private enough for you?"

"Certainly. Thank you for seeing me unannounced."

Crossing his arms, Jenkins rocked on his heels. "What can I do for you? You said it was important."

Basil rubbed his jaw. "Ah, yes. It's about Mrs. Hirsh. The young Mrs. Hirsch."

"Has something happened? Is she all right?"

"She's fine. I came to see you on her behalf. I understand the two of you have been walking out together." Basil narrowed his eyes. "You asked her to consider allowing you to court her."

Jenkins frowned. "That's between her and me."

"I'm involved now, and I need to know how serious you are." Basil stepped closer to the butcher. "Do you realize if you marry Rosa, you'll be responsible for her mother-in-law, too?"

"What?" The skin on Jenkins's face glistened, and he paled. "Is there some sort of law?"

"I take it you didn't think about that when you made your proposal to her."

"Why would I take on the elder Mrs. Hirsch? She's not related to Rosa. I'll ask you again. Is there a statute that says I have to burden myself with the old woman if I marry her daughter-in-law?"

"No, there's not a law requiring any such thing, but it's the right thing to do, Jenkins. She's widowed. And she lost both her sons. Rosa is the only family Noreen has left."

Jenkins head swung back and forth like a bull trapped in the ring. He pulled a handkerchief from his back pocket and mopped the sweat from his face. "It's too much to ask. I can't honestly say I care enough about Rosa to take on her mother-in-law. I have a mother of my own who requires care." He held his hands up in a gesture of surrender. "The young Mrs. Hirsch is all yours, Mr. Quincey. I'm assuming that's why you're *involved*. You want to marry the girl, well, you can have her." He pivoted and strode past the counter and behind the curtain. A door banged, and his footsteps faded.

Basil stared at the swaying cloth for a long moment then grinned. *Thank You, Lord. Thank You for paving the way for me to marry Rosa. I don't deserve it, but You have given me the desires of my heart. You are so good to me, Father.*

England, 1943

Epilogue

From deep within the house a baby cried, and Basil looked up toward the ceiling. Muffled footsteps hurried across the wooden floors overhead. Rosa's voice filtered down the stairs singing a German lullaby in her throaty alto tones. The sobbing ceased, and he imagined his wife sitting in the rocking chair, little Conrad nestled in her arms.

At first she refused to name their first-born after her deceased husband, but Basil knew it was the right thing to do. The man's life had been cut short before having children. He should have had a son, and now he did.

Basil sighed and picked up the newspaper. More than three years into the war, and headlines still shouted of battles lost and won. Casualty lists took up several pages. Photos of bombed-out cities glared at him.

He bowed his head and pinched the bridge of his nose.

"It's easier if you don't look." Noreen walked into the room on silent feet. "Edmund's mother taught me that, although I don't think she took her own advice while he was away."

Basil's head shot up. "I can't help myself. Rumors abound. At least I get some sense of what's occurring from the papers."

Noreen lowered herself on the couch and patted her graying hair. "But we can't do anything about it."

"We can pray."

She nodded. "Yes, we can always do that."

Basil folded the paper and tossed it on the table at his elbow. "I feel guilty, Noreen. Guilty that God has blessed me with a beautiful family, good health, and a successful business. I've done nothing to deserve it."

"None of us deserve what we have, Basil. God gives to whom he wishes. It is our job to accept it with joy and thankfulness and to share it with others." A shadow crossed her face. "I was bitter over the loss of my husband and my two sons. I turned my back on God, yet he blessed me with a second family. I, too, have done nothing to deserve it."

"God is good."

"Indeed he is."

The End

If you enjoyed *Love's Harvest*, please consider posting a review:

www.Amazon.com

www.Goodreads.com

Reading Group Guide for *Love's Harvest*

1. *Love's Harvest* is a modern retelling of the book of Ruth. How are Rosa and Noreen like Ruth and Naomi? How are they different?

2. Rosa left Germany and everything she knew to accompany her mother-in-law to England, a country at war with her homeland. Why do you think she did this? What kind of regrets might she have had about the move?

3. Rosa was misunderstood and mistreated by many people she came into contact with. Is this the same or different as Muslim's are experiencing in America today? How would you have reacted to having a citizen of Hitler's empire living in your country?

4. For what purpose did God work in the lives of Rosa, Noreen, and Basil? Name some ways God works in people's lives today. How has he worked in your life?

5. Discuss the characteristics of Basil. Discuss which of his characteristics are important to men today.

6. Discuss ways *Love's Harvest* points to better things to come through Jesus Christ.

7. What are lessons from this story you can apply to your own life?

Acknowledgements

Although writing a book is a solitary task, it is not a solitary journey. There have been many who have helped and encouraged me along the way.

My parents who presented me with my first writing tablet and encouraged me to capture my imagination with words. Thanks Mom and Dad!

Scribes212 – my ACFW on-line critique group: Marcy Dyer, Valerie Goree, Marcia Lahti, Catherine Leggitt, and the late Loretta Boyett (passed on to Glory, but never forgotten). Without your input, my writing would not be nearly as effective. (Where did I put that clue?)

My Wolfeboro critique group – we never did come up with a name! Helen Fernald, Cindy Scott, and Suzanne Simmons. Your feedback and encouragement have been invaluable.

Eva Marie Everson – my mentor/instructor with Christian Writers' Guild. You took a timid, untrained student and turned her into a writer. Many thanks!

SincNE, and the folks who coordinate the Crimebake Writing Conference. I have attended many writing conferences, but without a doubt, Crimebake is one of the best. Special thanks to Hank Phillippi Ryan, Halle Ephron, and Roberta Isleib for your encouragement and spot-on critiques of my work.

Tiger Wiseman – Thanks for providing the perfect writing get-away weekend. Your home is gorgeous, and you are the perfect hostess! Give Murphy a hug for me.

Joanne Balzer – For her German-speaking expertise. Thanks for ensuring I got it right!

My husband Wes deserves special kudos for understanding my need to write. Thank you for creating my writing room – it's perfect, and I'm thankful for it every day. Thank you for your willingness to accept a house that's a bit cluttered, laundry that's not always done, and meals on the go. I love you.

And finally, to God be the glory. I thank him for giving me the gift of writing and the inspiration to tell stories that shine the light on his goodness and mercy.

ABOUT THE AUTHOR

A freelance writer for over ten years, Linda Shenton Matchett has had a wide and varied career that includes stints as a Human Resources professional, youth center director, B&B owner, and dining services manager. She loves history of all kinds, and serves as a volunteer docent at the Wright Museum of WWII. A member of Sisters in Crime and ACFW, Linda writes World War II and mystery fiction. She was a semi-finalist in ACFW's 2013 and 2015 Genesis contests. She makes her home in New Hampshire's Lakes Region with her husband Wes and fur-baby, Ben.

Visit her website: www.LindaShentonMatchett.com

Facebook: www.facebook.com/LindaShentonMatchettAuthor

Pinterest: www.pinterest.com/lindasmatchett

LinkedIn: www.linkedin.com/in/authorlindamatchett